MAGIC

IN

LIGHT

BOOKS BY KRISTA STREET
SUPERNATURAL WORLD NOVELS

Fae of Snow & Ice

Court of Winter

Thorns of Frost

Wings of Snow

Crowns of Ice

Supernatural Curse

Wolf of Fire

Bound of Blood

Cursed of Moon

Forged of Bone

Supernatural Institute

Fated by Starlight

Born by Moonlight

Hunted by Firelight

Kissed by Shadowlight

Supernatural Community

Magic in Light

Power in Darkness

Dragons in Fire

Angel in Embers

Supernatural Standalones

Beast of Shadows

MAGIC
IN
LIGHT

paranormal shifter romance

SUPERNATURAL COMMUNITY
BOOK ONE

KRISTA STREET

PREFACE

Magic in Light is a coming-of-age paranormal shifter romance and is the first book in the *Supernatural Community* series. The recommended reading age is 18+.

CHAPTER ONE

The menacing words from the email stared back at me.

Dear Ms. Gresham,

Your time on this earth is ticking, witch. You'll be dead by the end of the month. Tick tock. Tick tock.

Your biggest fan.

"Daria?"

My head lifted from my laptop at the sound of my manager's voice.

Cecile appeared behind me in the dressing room mirror. "Your new bodyguard is here." Her gray hair swept back from her face in a matronly bun. Worry lines tightened her mouth, making her lips pucker.

Since this was the third death threat I'd received this

week, I could understand her concern. I craned my neck to see around her. "Is he with you?"

"He's waiting outside. I wanted to make sure you were ready to see him."

"Yeah, I'm ready." I pushed back my chair, the legs catching on the thin carpet.

"You can stay here, Dar. I'll bring him in."

Before I could protest, Cecile exited the tiny dressing room in our travel bus. The cheap brown paint covering the door peeled away from the surface, and the worn carpet had faded from years of too much sunlight. However, the bus ran and that was more important than any cosmetic appeal.

With trembling fingers, I closed my laptop, but when I tried to set it aside, it nearly fell from my shaky grip.

"Crap," I whispered.

After muttering a spell under my breath, my laptop lifted in the air, my telekinetic magic holding it aloft. It glided to where I stored it by the desk and landed safely on the scarred wood shelf.

Forcing myself to take deep, steadying breaths, I peered out the window, hoping to catch a peek of my new bodyguard before he climbed aboard the bus.

But when I cracked the blinds, there was no sign of him. What I did see was a lone gas station across the road. Racks of junk food and miscellaneous paraphernalia filled the windows. Behind the gas station lay endless plains and a sky bathed in red.

We had pulled off some highway in rural southern

Kansas, the scheduled pickup place to meet my bodyguard. I didn't know the exact location. Tomorrow, we would be in western Nebraska after Mike drove us through the night.

I let the blinds fall back into place and plopped onto the chair. My bright turquoise eyes stared back at me in the dressing room mirror, reflecting my worried mood. *Just calm down, Dar.*

But that was easier said than done. Whoever my new guard was would be the first bodyguard I'd ever employed. Until recently, I'd never needed one.

I studied myself and smiled sadly. The image staring back at me looked like a younger version of my mother. For centuries, my mother's people had birthed only daughters, and we all looked similar—golden hair, startling turquoise eyes, pale skin, and small frames.

If I ever had a daughter, she would be a near replica of me, and it wouldn't be just my looks she would inherit. She would also acquire my telekinetic magic and my healing light. My magic, I could hide and only use when needed, but my healing light was my purpose.

A purpose my mother and my nan had shared.

I hung my head. *I miss you both so much.*

The door to the dressing room squeaked open, startling me. Cecile appeared in the doorway, her hands clasped tightly in front of her. A few wispy strands of gray hair had escaped her normally tamed bun.

"Daria, this is Logan Smith." Cecile sidestepped, revealing a tall, dark-haired man behind her.

My breath caught in my throat.

He had to be at least six-three, and his shoulders were so broad they brushed the doorway. Thick dark hair covered his head. His complexion was unblemished, his features chiseled, and a large duffel bag hung over his shoulder.

I swallowed my rush of awareness for how very . . . *male* . . . he was. *Wow.* I had no idea he would be so good looking.

Shaking myself, I stood to greet him.

According to Cecile, Logan Smith was twenty-five years old—four years older than I was—and had over six years of experience in security and came from a military background. He also came with a glowing resume and had passed his background check with flying colors. From here on, he would be traveling with us.

And hopefully keeping me safe so I can continue my supernatural-healing tour.

I held out my hand, knowing it would activate my gift but doing it anyway. "It's nice to meet you. I'm Daria Gresham."

I tensed, waiting for his touch. Once our skin connected, my healing light would escape from the chest I buried it in deep within my belly. Unlike my telekinetic magic, my healing light had proved unruly. The only times I willingly let my light out was during my healing sessions, but touch triggered it despite my attempts to control it. A handshake with Logan guaranteed that unpleasant sparks would shoot up my arms once we made contact.

4

Still, social niceties required certain interactions, so I usually dealt with the unpleasant aftermath touch elicited. Besides, handshakes only lasted a second or two. Anyone could handle a second or two of pain.

Logan's hand engulfed mine, his palm rough and warm. "Nice to meet you, too, although I wish the circumstances were different."

My lungs seized, rendering speech impossible. I cringed. Waiting.

Logan pumped my hand once, twice, then . . . he let go.

The sparks never came.

"Cecile's told me you need protection." Logan's brown eyes grew alight with concern.

Frowning, I let my arm fall back to my side. "Um . . . yeah, that's right. I've been receiving death threats for the past few weeks." I eyed his hand again. *Did I really not respond to him?* Shaking myself, I added, "And thanks for answering our ad and coming on such short notice. Cecile tells me you were formerly in the military but now do freelance work?"

"That's right. I've been working personal security for a few years."

My gaze unwillingly returned to his hand again. *How come I didn't respond?*

Cecile gave me a curious look before waving toward the bunk beds in the back. "The plan is for you to stay with us on the bus."

Logan hoisted his duffel bag higher. "That's what I'm counting on. I can't do my job if I'm not close."

Cecile stepped forward. "If you'll follow me, I can show you where to set your things."

Logan gave me a small smile then trailed behind Cecile from the dressing room. I stepped to the doorway to watch, my frown deepening.

Logan showed no outward reaction to our bus's grim interior on his way to the back. Even though our home on the road was clean, it was old. More than one visitor had wrinkled their noses at it.

I nibbled my lip and, against my better judgment, allowed myself a moment to study him. Faded, sturdy boots covered his feet. They were the kind of boots that would allow him to run at a moment's notice but also plant a firm kick. Worn jeans hugged his lean waist and firm backside.

His fitted dark T-shirt awarded me a view of his strong back muscles bunching and tightening beneath the thin material when he moved. I bit my lip more, my stomach tightening. *Damn, he's hot.*

But as soon as that thought came, I shook it off. He was also my employee, and I'd hired him for his competence, not his good looks.

What the heck's the matter with you, Dar?

I returned to the desk to ponder my reaction, or rather non-reaction, to Logan's touch. I figured it was a fluke, but the sight of my closed laptop on the scarred wooden shelf made any curiosity about my new bodyguard disappear.

My heart pounded, the staccato feeling growing more

common every day. *"Your time on this earth is ticking, witch. You'll be dead by the end of the month."*

"Daria?" Cecile's voice carried from the back of the bus. "Logan wants to speak to you."

I shook off my thoughts and slipped my shoes on before retreating to where Cecile and Logan waited by the bunks. I passed the two couches at the front, along with the kitchen and the tiny table that could seat four since the bunks lay in the back. Our home was small, cramped at times, but it fulfilled our needs.

The carpet slid under my feet, and my stomach fluttered the closer I got to Logan. There was just something . . . about him.

Logan stepped to the side to make room for me when I approached. I had to tilt my head back to meet his gaze. The top of my head barely reached his collarbone. The fluttering in my stomach increased just as the hiss of the door came from the front.

Mike jumped up the stairs. "Are we ready to hit the road?" His bushy black hair rested on his shoulders, hanging down from beneath his baseball cap. He'd worn the same New York Yankees cap for the past nineteen years.

"Excuse me." Cecile bustled past Logan and me on her way to the front. "Yes, Mike. We're ready to go. I just want to review our itinerary one more time."

Mike rolled his eyes and chuckled. "Yes, yes . . . I figured you would." When he caught me watching him, he winked.

I smothered a smile and Logan cocked an eyebrow. I

hurried to explain my amusement. "Cecile micromanages everything, and if she ever does it to you, don't take it personally. She's like that with everyone."

"Good to know." He scratched his jaw, and a moment of silence passed while Cecile and Mike's soft conversation drifted to us. Logan dropped his hand and leaned against his bunk. "Do you employ both of them as well or are they related to you?"

"No, they're not related, but I consider them family. Cecile was my mother's best friend and is like a second mom to me."

When Logan's gaze didn't waver, I added, "She's also very dedicated to her job and is fiercely protective of everything involved in my healing tour. She books the clients I see, keeps us on schedule, makes sure I eat, and all that stuff. She's super organized, and honestly, I would be lost without her. Essentially, she's the perfect manager."

A lock of dark hair fell across Logan's forehead. "Ah, your manager. That explains it, and I kind of suspected she was organized given my interview with her. If she ever decides to find a new career, she should consider joining the Marines."

I laughed, the sound startling me. Given all that had transpired since the death threats began, I couldn't remember the last time I'd laughed.

Logan's eyes twinkled. "And what about Mike? Is he the driver?"

"Yeah. Mike's similar to Cecile. He's not a relation, but he's been in my life for as long as I can remember."

Logan lifted an arm to prop against his bunk. His bicep bulged.

Damn. So. Hot.

For a moment, I stood there tongue-tied before mentally slapping myself and saying in a rush, "So yeah, a long time ago, my mom healed Mike's mother in a session, but he didn't have the money to pay her, so he offered to drive us for a few months, and a few months turned into nineteen years. He's known me since I was a baby, and he's kind of like a father to me—"

I clamped my mouth shut. *Why was I still talking?* I sounded like a blubbering moron, but Logan merely watched me with an amused twinkle in his eyes.

I gave him a weak smile. "So both Cecile and Mike are kind of like family to me—the only family I have now."

"And your healing tours, what are those? I take it that's where I'll be guarding you?"

"Yep, exactly." I twisted my hands.

Seriously, stand still!

Forcing my arms back to my sides, I added, "The tours are my job. My entire life's work is dedicated to healing those who are chronically or terminally ill. I use my gift to cure them."

I tensed, waiting for his reaction. Those who didn't believe in my light assumed I was a fraud, taking advantage of the weak and depraved. And I never spoke of or demonstrated my telekinetic magic. That would garner too much attention, never mind that my spells were something I rarely used anyway. The Gresham women's focus had always been on our healing light.

But the judgmental, scornful look that I'd grown accustomed to seeing in strangers' eyes never materialized in Logan's, but the twinkle in his gaze faded, his expression turning serious again. "I'll do my best to keep you safe so you can continue working. Now, should we sit? I'd like to hear more about what's happened and why you've hired me."

I picked at my fingers again, despite telling myself not to, and nodded toward the dressing room. "You can have a look for yourself. According to the latest threat, I'll be dead within the month."

CHAPTER TWO

When I turned to guide Logan back to the dressing room, my mouth parted. Mike and Cecile stood immobile at the front of the bus. They stared in our direction, no doubt having heard our entire exchange. Panic covered Cecile's face. She'd been looking that way all month.

When Cecile stepped my way, I subtly shook my head. I knew she wanted to ask Logan if going to the police was the best course of action. Mike felt the same, but I'd been fighting them on it for weeks and didn't feel like getting into it.

Gresham women never turned to the law for a reason.

"This way," I said to Logan.

The scent of stale coffee hung in the air when we passed the kitchen. None of us had cleaned the coffee pot yet. Once we stood in the dressing room, Logan's forearm brushed mine in the cramped space.

I jumped back, out of habit more than anything, before my gift could activate.

Logan raised an eyebrow. "You okay?"

"Yep, fine." I forced a smile. It was not the time to explain that random touch always caused my healing light to escape from my internal storage chest.

Logan's large muscled arm reached for my laptop. "Is this your computer?"

"That's the one."

He picked it up. When the screen popped up for my password, he handed it over. I quickly typed it in, which got a heavy scowl from him.

"Remind me to teach you about using secure passwords."

My jaw dropped. "You saw my password?"

"No, I didn't watch, but considering it's only four characters, I already know it's not secure." He took the laptop from me and pulled out the lone chair, indicating for me to sit down.

So he's incredibly observant. Good to know.

I perched awkwardly on the chair's edge while Logan stood with my laptop in hand. Given that my email pulled up as soon as the internet was open, I didn't need to log in.

He grumbled when he saw that. "The first thing we're doing is having Internet Safety 101."

I rolled my eyes. "Yeah, I know my stuff isn't very secure, but I've never had to worry about security before."

His dark eyebrows drew together. "Everybody needs to worry about security in the world we live in."

An edge filled his tone, making me think he'd seen his fair share of what those threats were.

Logan scanned the latest email. "When did you get this?"

"This morning. It's the third one this week, and they're always from different email addresses."

"And is this your personal email? Or your work email?"

"My personal. Cecile handles my work email. Only I have access to this one."

"Have you replied to any of these?"

"No. Never."

"And do you have any idea who this could be? Do you have any enemies or know of someone who would want to hurt you?"

Clasping my shaky hands, I replied, "No. Not that I know of."

He scanned the message again. "Are you sure your personal email isn't shared somewhere online? Even the Dark Web?"

I drew in a ragged breath. "I don't know. I don't think so, but I've had it for a few years, so . . . maybe?" I shrugged helplessly. The entire situation made me feel exactly that—helpless. It wasn't something I was used to feeling, and I sure as hell didn't like it.

Logan crouched at my side and tilted the laptop for me to see. His scent drifted my way—sandalwood and foliage. He smelled like the woods after a light rain. It was a strangely alluring smell. "You said you've had three threats this week?"

I cleared my throat and sat up straighter. "Yes, three. I've kept all of them in this folder, here." I pointed at it on the screen. "I've had a dozen total."

He opened the folder, studying each message. "All from different emails, but we can still check the IP addresses. Although if this person has any idea what he's doing, there won't be a way to trace him."

"Him? You think it's definitely a male?"

Logan pulled up the first email again. "I think so. Each message is concise with short sentences. That's typical of men. And you see how he begins and ends each message with the same greeting and ending? It's most likely the same person who wrote each message. He's using different email addresses to hide."

My hands shook less at Logan's calm logic. "That makes sense."

He closed my laptop. "Mind if I keep this? We'll need to change your passcode so I can log in, but I have a friend who can run a check on the email addresses. And when this creep messages you again, I want to know immediately. Are you expecting emails from anyone else?"

I shook my head. "No. I don't get many. Most of the people who need to contact me are on this bus."

His head cocked. In the dying light, his features looked even more chiseled. He was truly striking. "No women you keep in touch with or a boyfriend you're expecting to hear from?"

My cheeks heated when he said *boyfriend*. "No—to both of your questions."

I held my breath as I waited for Logan to say we should go to the police now that he knew what we were dealing with.

But instead, Logan simply replied, "I have a few ideas for how to deal with this perp. I'll let you know if anything that you need to see comes in." He took a step toward the door, so I hastily stood to follow.

"Will you let me know when his next email arrives?" I tried to mask the panic in my tone, but it still crept through.

When he turned to face me, my breath caught. His deep-set chocolate-brown eyes held a fierce determination, and his firm lips tightened, giving me a hint of the steel backbone hidden within him. For a brief moment, I saw a glimpse of something inside Logan Smith that promised retribution for anyone who crossed him.

Strangely enough, I found that glimpse comforting instead of frightening.

"You don't need to be scared. I'll keep you safe, but if you'd like to know when he contacts you again, yes, I'll tell you."

"Thank you."

Cecile appeared in the doorway as the bus engine started, a low rumble that always reminded me of thunder. The dim light penetrating the closed blinds told me the sun had nearly set.

"We're heading out now since it's an eight-hour drive." Cecile's bun, firmly back in place, sat at the nape of her neck, the wispy tendrils gone. "Do either of you need anything before we get moving?"

I shook my head. "I'm fine, and I just finished showing Logan the messages. He's caught up for the time being."

Cecile's mouth tightened, the worry lines reappearing. "I sure hope you keep my girl safe."

Standing as he was, all six-three of him with his thick muscles, square jaw, and firm lips, he made my heart flutter again.

"I'll keep her safe. You have my word."

Cecile let out a breath just as the bus began to move. "Thank goodness."

The bus shifted forward. I swayed but righted myself.

"Off we go!" Mike called cheerfully from the front.

Bustling out of the room, Cecile called over her shoulder, "How about I make everyone a bite to eat? We've got a long drive ahead of us, and tomorrow's a big day. Ooh, and from the smell of it, that coffee pot needs to be cleaned!"

As Cecile worked in the kitchen, Mike whistled a tune to the radio. I was left in the doorway of the small dressing room with Logan only feet away.

"I'll grab clean sheets for your bed, and—"

The bus abruptly lurched as Mike turned us onto the highway. I fell forward and collided with Logan, my body planting against his.

I sucked in a breath when his hands automatically grasped my arms to keep me from falling. At his touch, I closed my eyes, readying myself for the feel of my healing light escaping.

A second passed. It was enough time to activate my gift.

Another second passed.

Nothing.

The lid to the chest where I sealed my light didn't even crack. Not one electric jolt or painful flare followed. All I felt were warm, calloused hands holding my upper arms while a hard male chest pressed against me protectively, almost cradling me.

My lips parted, my breath rushing out.

I tilted my head up to see Logan staring down at me. His Adam's apple bobbed when he swallowed.

My boobs were crushed against his chest. I felt every hard line of him. I'd never experienced anything like it. That was the first time I'd ever touched a man and felt nothing but *him*.

Logan abruptly let go and stepped back, a shallow breath lifting his chest.

A chill settled on my arms from where his hands had been. My mouth parted. *So earlier wasn't a fluke?* My jaw dropped even more as that implication set in.

A country song drifted to my ears. Mike had turned the radio up. Banging came from the kitchen, only a few yards away, as Cecile did the dishes.

I widened the distance between Logan and me, stepping into the hall. "I'll just go see if Cecile needs any help."

Logan cleared his throat and raked a hand through his hair. "Right. No problem. I'll . . . uh . . . contact that friend of mine."

"Yeah. Sure." I hurried from the room, my long hair

flowing behind me. Once out of view, I didn't stop at Cecile's side. Instead, I ran to the very back of the bus and locked myself in the bathroom.

I sank to the floor, my mind reeling as reality set in. My breath came out in ragged pants. *Did that really just happen?* Because as much as I wanted to deny what had just occurred between Logan and me, I couldn't.

That only meant one thing. My mother was right.

Mates did exist.

CHAPTER THREE

"We should get to bed, Dar." Cecile's voice penetrated the bathroom's hollow wood door, which was so flimsy it sounded as if she were in the room with me.

With a shaky hand, I set my toothbrush down on the sink. "I know. I'll be out in a minute."

Her retreating footsteps tapped on the other side.

I rinsed my mouth then wiped the steam from the mirror. Turquoise eyes stared back at me, and wet hair dripped down my back. Even though I didn't need one, I'd showered anyway, doing anything to pass time as I hid in the bathroom *again* following dinner.

We had only been on the road for two hours, yet it had felt like an eternity. I kept thinking about that contact I'd shared with Logan—the contact in which my gift didn't activate for a second time, which solidified that he was a potential mate.

The first potential mate I'd ever met.

Ever since that moment, I'd been a jumbled mess. Between my mumbled, nearly unintelligible conversation, and my fluttering hands and fidgeting, I was sure Logan had noticed my erratic behavior, but he hadn't said anything. Thankfully, after Cecile made dinner, Logan had retreated to the front of the bus to do stuff on my laptop. I stayed in the back.

Still, I'd felt like a pacing animal at the zoo since discovering what my bodyguard could be.

My fingers trembled when I picked up my hairbrush. I winced when I pulled it too quickly through my damp hair and it caught in a snarl. Around me, toiletry items vibrated on their shelves, creating a buzzing in the bathroom as the bus rumbled beneath my soles. I steadied the cup on the sink so it wouldn't fall.

"Daria?"

I jumped at the sound of Logan's deep voice through the door.

His soft knock came next. "Are you all right? You've been in there awhile."

"Fine. Sorry. I'll be out soon!"

Heat rushed up my neck, spreading over my face like a bad rash. I'd been in the bathroom for over an hour. No doubt, Logan thought I was some kind of pretty girl, primping and preening in front of the mirror when the reality couldn't be further from that.

A quick look around the tiny bathroom had me groaning. In my haste to escape my bodyguard's presence, I'd forgotten to bring in a change of clothes. Normally, Mike, Cecile, and I would walk to the dressing room wrapped in a towel following a shower, since that was where we stored our clothes, but with Logan on the bus now . . .

Just be quick about it. I cinched my towel tightly around my chest and opened the door.

What greeted me on the other side made my heart stop. Logan stood in the doorway. Apparently, he hadn't retreated to the front of the bus yet.

Of course he didn't, Dar! You never heard him walk away!

"Oh!" My eyes widened as I tightened the towel more. "I didn't realize you were still here."

His gaze dipped for a fraction of a second to my breasts, which practically spilled over the top of my towel, before he jerked his head upright.

My cheeks warmed more. "Um . . . I'll just get dressed. Excuse me."

Logan turned stiffly to let me pass. He seemed intent on keeping his attention above my head. "I didn't mean to rush you."

"That's okay. You didn't. Honestly, I was almost done."

I hurried past him before he could respond. When I reached the dressing room, I peeked in his direction.

He still stood in the hall outside the bathroom. From that distance, I couldn't be sure, but his expression seemed strained. With a shake of his head, almost as if he were talking to himself, he ducked into the bathroom and closed the door.

DESPITE THE RUMBLING bus lulling me to sleep that night as we headed toward my next show, I tossed and turned. Dreams of evil men running, searching, and wanting plagued me. I knew it stemmed from the death threats, and I also knew that discovering Logan was a potential mate heightened every other emotion I felt.

I grumbled and turned onto my side. Soft country music floated down from the front of the bus. A few times, Mike hummed or sang along as he drove through the night. Below me, Cecile's soft breathing floated up, and across the aisle, Logan's broad back faced me.

My gaze traveled over his shadowed form, haltingly, curiously. His muscles strained against his thin shirt, leaving little to the imagination. A surreal feeling floated through me.

If I were to reach across the aisle and touch him, all I would feel were those hard planes and sinewy muscles.

If I slipped my hand under his shirt, his heat would warm my palm.

If I nuzzled into his neck, his scent would fill my nose. I could press kisses into the base of his throat while his steel-like arms enclosed around me, and all I would feel was *him*, nothing else, nothing more.

Just him.

I abruptly turned and stared at the ceiling, my breath coming out in harsh pants as a new pulsing sensation grew between my thighs. I squeezed my eyes tightly shut, reminding myself of my mother's words.

Mom warned you. She said if you ever meet a potential mate, your body will tell you. I wanted to punch something. *But does it have to be my bodyguard? Someone I'm employing?*

Granted, I didn't know Logan very well, if at all, yet he struck me as someone who took his job seriously. I couldn't imagine him crossing the line between professional freelancer and a hot one-night stand while still working for me.

Sighing heavily, I forced my attention out the narrow window just above my bunk. A black sky stretched to the horizon, a thousand stars glittering in the cavernous sky. Every now and then, bright lights marred the beauty when we passed an interstate exit with overhead lights.

I pulled the sheets up higher, the soft cotton smooth along my skin. With a regretful shake of my head, I turned on my side.

As soon as we caught the psychopath stalking me, Logan Smith would be on his way. It was best to remember that and stuff these new sensations down as far as they would go. Because Logan Smith was not here to find a girlfriend. He was here to do a job, and that was it.

BY THE TIME the sun rose, I'd managed to fall back to sleep so I wasn't a complete zombie when I woke for the second time. However, when I rolled onto my back and pushed long locks of hair from my eyes, the last thing I expected to hear was a deep voice rumbling by my ear.

"Do you want a cup of coffee? I just made a pot."

My eyes flashed open. Logan stood beside my bed with two steaming cups of coffee in hand. The hazelnut scent drifted my way.

"Oh!" I pulled the covers up higher. They'd bunched down around my waist, a flash of my bare abdomen peeking out.

I sat up and straightened my shirt. Cecile's bed lay vacant beneath me. Only Logan and I occupied the back since Cecile sat near Mike, keeping him company as he drove.

I pushed the hair from my face and reached for the mug. "Thanks. What time is it?"

"Just past eight. Mike said we'll be at your next venue in twenty minutes."

"And that friend of yours who's good with computers? Have you heard from him?"

"He's still on assign—" Logan raked a hand through his hair. "Not yet. I'm sure I'll hear from him soon, though."

On assignment? Is that what he was going to say? On assignment for what?

I brushed that thought off and curled my fingers more tightly around the cup, trying to ignore the tingling deep in my belly at how near he stood.

Logan's jaw clenched, and he shifted his attention higher above my head. It was only then I realized my breasts were straining against my T-shirt since I didn't wear a bra to bed.

With burning cheeks, I turned slightly. First my exposed midriff, then my boobs were demanding attention.

Must find a baggy T-shirt to wear at night—preferably a long baggy T-shirt. Maybe one with holes in it, or an unattractive coffee stain, or perhaps overalls. Surely, they're not that uncomfortable to sleep in.

Logan cleared his throat and took a step back. "I'll head back up front. Why don't you join me after you're dressed and we can talk about what today will bring?"

"Sure." The flush on my cheeks grew. "Just give me ten minutes, and I'll be right up."

Logan's heavy footsteps filled the bus. I waited until he'd moved a safe distance away before I slid off my bunk, careful not to spill the coffee, then grabbed a change of clothes and darted into the bathroom.

Just as I was about to close the bathroom door, Cecile and Mike's soft conversation drifted my way.

From the snippets I caught, I knew Cecile was going through the day's plan with Mike. Once we reached our venue, we would have a lot to do before my new clients arrived. On show days, Mike usually didn't sleep until noon despite driving all night. He never complained, though.

I firmly closed the bathroom door and groaned when I saw my image in the mirror. Not only were my nipples standing tall and proud for the world to see, but my long blond hair was also the epitome of bed head. Wild hair tangled around my shoulders, and my lips were slightly swollen.

Anxiously, I set my coffee down on the basin. The hazelnut fragrance filled the cramped space.

I grabbed a brush and got to work on my hair. I looked like I'd just woken up from a roll in the hay with my boyfriend. Never mind that I was a virgin.

After washing my face and twirling my hair into a loose bun, I threw on a pair of jeans, a bra that holstered the girls firmly in place, and a T-shirt. Leaving my feet bare, I grabbed my coffee and left the bathroom to join everyone else at the front of the bus.

Logan stood stiffly when I approached. Being in his presence made the fluttering in my stomach begin anew, but I pushed it down.

Someone's threatening your life, Dar. Perhaps keep that in mind, hmm?

I took a sip of the coffee, spilling a bit over the side in my haste to get it to my lips.

"Oh, Dar, you're up!" Cecile hurried to my side and looked me over. "You look well rested. That's good. I know how taxing these days can be." She glanced at her watch. "We'll only have an hour to set up if we also want to make breakfast. Mike ran into some unforeseen road construction along the way, so we're running a little late, but don't worry. We'll make do, just like always."

I nodded and took another sip of coffee, trying to ignore the imposing hulk of Logan beside me. *How is it possible that he's so big?* Just his presence practically created gravitational pull. He was like two hundred twenty pounds of solid muscle that appeared as hard as granite.

Taking too big a gulp of coffee, I winced when it burned my throat. "How many are on the schedule today?"

"We have twenty-two—"

"Twenty-two?" My eyebrows shot to my hairline.

"I know. It'll be tight, but with thirty minutes each, we can get it done. I know that's more than you normally like, but a few of these people have been trying to see you for over two years." Cecile continued talking in her fluttery way. "The first arrives at ten. We'll break for lunch at three before starting again at four. The last arrives at nine thirty, so we should be wrapping up a little after ten tonight."

"That's a lot. I hope I can perform and don't get too tired."

Cecile placed a comforting hand on my shoulder. Her palm caused a warm sensation to slide underneath my skin, like the sun's rays warming my back. She withdrew her hand before those rays turned into electric jolts, like lightning before a storm. After living with me for my entire life, she knew my body's limits. "If you need to rest in between sessions, we'll arrange it. Your clients can wait if need be."

Logan's eyebrows drew together. "Who are these twenty-two people?"

Cecile laced her fingers. "Most are elderly with life-threatening diagnoses, a few middle-aged people, two children with advanced cancer, and one troubled teen who has the beginning symptoms of schizophrenia."

"So it could essentially be anyone that's meeting Daria today?"

Goose bumps rose along my arms. Logan seemed to think my stalker could be a client.

"No, not anyone." Cecile shook her head. "These are all people who've been eagerly trying to see Daria for months, some for years. Many of them are traveling hundreds of miles for a session with her."

"But it could still be anyone," Logan persisted. "What criteria do they have to meet to see her? I know it's not all related to how much money they have."

"Correct." Cecile nodded. "We only charge what people can afford, but we do require proof of their illnesses. Usually, that would be documents from physicians outlining their diagnoses, but if they're not able to provide that, we require testimonials from friends, family, and neighbors of the individual, stating they've been gravely ill."

Logan's eyebrows shot up. "Testimonials? So, essentially, anyone can see her if they pay a few people to state there's something medically wrong with them?"

My shoulders hunched as Logan pointed out our lack of security.

Cecile frowned. "Hardly. Many of them have to wait months to see Daria, and those that aren't seriously ill usually give up if they're looking for easy access."

"Stalkers don't usually give up easily." Logan placed his

hands on his hips. "What kind of security do you have at this venue?"

Her hands fluttered nervously to her hair. "Um . . . we don't."

"Security isn't provided by the venue?"

Cecile and I shared worried looks.

"Today, it's not really a venue," I replied. "So to speak. Usually, we rent a small building or commission a tent at a county fair, but things have changed since the . . . threats started. What we're doing now is a little unconventional."

Logan scowled heavily. If a thunderstorm could represent a person's expression, Logan's would be it. "How unconventional?"

"We're not advertising where Daria will be anymore," Cecile replied, "and we've taken to using unusual facilities to meet. Today, we're arriving at a farmer's old barn off a barren highway. Her next show will be held in the back room of a magic shop in a small town in Wyoming. We're using small venues to keep a lower profile."

Skepticism swam in his dark eyes. "And how many people know about today's location?"

My heart pounded again. Words from yesterday's email sprang to my mind. *Tick tock. Tick tock.* I took a deep breath before saying, "Only the people I'm seeing today. Cecile contacted them yesterday and told them where to meet us. They've given their word they won't tell anyone."

Logan cupped the back of his neck and sighed in exasperation. "Their word. Right."

Though Cecile looked as if she wanted to say more, Mike cut in.

"The barn's just up ahead. About a minute out." His cheerful voice was a complete contradiction to the tension radiating off Logan.

I ducked my head to peek out the front windshield. Ahead, wheat fields surrounded the barren highway, and a lone rundown barn jutted up between the tall stalks about a quarter mile off the road. Off in the distance, a farmer worked a field. Other than that, I didn't see anyone.

"That's where you're meeting your clients today?" Logan frowned.

I shrugged apologetically. "Welcome to the life of a supernatural healer who someone wants burned at the stake."

CHAPTER FOUR

I grimaced, watching the tension build in Logan like a tightly coiled spring. He paced up and down the length of the bus. Seeing his worry made guilt bite me hard. Trying to hide our locations wasn't the best response to my stalker's threats. I knew that, but none of us knew what else to do.

Mike slowed the bus, the scent of burning brakes filling the cab, just before he turned us off the highway to follow the gravel road up to the barn.

Outside, the sky was an endless blue, not a cloud to be seen. Summer's grip didn't seem to be lessening as the end of August neared.

When we stopped, the brakes hissed. A plume of dust from the gravel road swirled around the windows.

To the right, a derelict barn loomed through the dusty cloud. It teetered menacingly to one side. I only hoped it remained standing for another twelve hours. Given how rundown it appeared, that was questionable.

"We're here!" Mike stood, his paunch belly stretching over his jeans.

Cecile licked her lips nervously as she assessed the decrepit structure. "We'll just start setting up then. Set up takes a while."

Logan moved in front of her before she could exit the bus. "At least tell me the clients meeting Daria today are vetted."

"Vetted?" I asked. "What do you mean by that?"

"Are background checks completed? Or, at the very least, are they searched before they're allowed near her? Will they be allowed to bring bags in? How many people are allowed with her at the same time? What process do you use to keep her safe?"

Cecile and I shared more apprehensive looks before I replied, "We honestly haven't had any incidents in the past month, despite the threats. Sure, some family members become upset if I can't see their loved one, but Mike usually deals with them. For the most part, we've been lucky."

Worry lines creased Logan's forehead. "I don't operate on luck."

SINCE WE'D ALREADY PROCURED the necessary permits to run my "farm stand" from the local authorities, and since the landowner had agreed to let us rent his barn for the day, Logan seemed a little more at ease that we were legal, but still . . .

The energy surrounding him was akin to a bomb about to detonate. His hands clenched and unclenched as he helped set up the portable chairs for family members and the bed for my clients. Tension oozed from his shoulders when we set out the snacks and drinks for my clients who regularly traveled hundreds of miles to see me. Logan continually stalked past the barn doors as we spread cloths over the furniture and set out candles with calming scents of lavender and rosemary.

He looked as if he needed the calming scents more than anyone.

But despite his prickly energy, I still noticed the broad length of his shoulders and how his dark hair ruffled in the wind. Every time he moved, my senses perked up, begging me to take note of his strong hands and hard physique. Logan was still a potential mate, and my body seemed intent on not letting me forget that.

After everything was ready, I hurried back to the bus, committed to putting some much needed distance between Logan Smith and me.

In the small kitchen, Cecile was busy preparing a late breakfast. She already had the bread out and bacon sizzled in a pan, the fragrant scent filling the bus.

I grabbed the bread. "Need help?"

Her eyebrows drew together when I dropped a slice on the counter. "Everything okay?"

"Yeah, just nervous about the show." I placed a few pieces of bread into the toaster before locating the butter on the counter.

Cecile eyed me again, reminding me of the knowing looks my mother used to give me. "Your cheeks are rosy. Show days don't make your cheeks rosy." She flipped the bacon, grease splattering over the pan's sides.

"They are?" I scowled in disgust that my emotions were so clearly on display.

"Are you going to tell me what's going on? I know whatever's bothering you isn't about your upcoming show." She turned to face me, planting a hand on her hip. "You've been tense ever since last night."

I began cracking eggs into a bowl before whisking them a little too briskly.

She sighed. "Dar, what's up?"

With a huff, I set the bowl down and fiddled with the blinds over the kitchen window, peering through a crack. Logan and Mike had moved from the barn to stand outside. Midmorning sunshine streamed down on them.

I let the blinds fall back into place. "Logan touched me briefly last night when I fell into him after Mike turned the bus sharply, but my gift didn't activate."

Her lips parted. "It didn't?"

"No. That's the first time that's ever happened." I grabbed another pan for the eggs and flipped on the stove's second burner.

Cecile's expression turned pensive as she turned back to the bacon. "So he's a—"

"No. Don't say it." I dropped a dollop of butter into the pan and slid it around before adding the eggs.

She covered my hand with hers when I began to stir the eggs. Her touch elicited a small response from my gift, but I stuffed the lid to my internal storage chest down just as she removed her hand.

"You know what your mother said about touch when you find—"

"I know, but he's my *bodyguard*, and I'm his employer! He can't be . . . you know. Besides, he probably has a girl-friend. I mean, look at him." I cracked the blinds again. We were rewarded with a view of Logan's broad shoulders and firm backside.

Cecile shrugged. "True, he may have a girlfriend, and while I don't fully understand how your gift works in that aspect, I *do* know what your mom said about potential mates."

I sagged against the counter. "But he'll be gone as soon as this stalker stuff is cleared up."

Her expression turned sympathetic as she grabbed the plates. "Maybe, Dar. But what if he doesn't have a girl-friend and he can turn into so much more?"

MY KNEE BOUNCED all throughout breakfast. I tried to concentrate on the salty bacon and buttery toast, but my body had other ideas.

Every time Logan bit into his food, I wanted to watch

the strong muscles of his jaw. And every time a breeze drifted across our makeshift picnic as we sat outside on lawn chairs, his tantalizing scent made my nose twitch.

Thankfully, Logan sat over two feet away so we had no chance of accidentally touching.

Still, my gaze kept drifting his way.

About halfway through breakfast, a buzz sounded from Logan's pocket. He pulled out his cell phone, and I couldn't help but glance at it. A name flashed across the top of a text.

Crystal.

I only caught a few words in my hasty glance.

. . . miss you. When can you call? I've been . . .

My cheeks flushing, I snapped my head away as a swell of disappointment rose so strongly in me I almost choked.

Logan's jaw tightened when he read Crystal's message. His fingers moved hesitantly, almost reluctantly, as he typed in a short reply before shoving the phone back into his pocket.

I watched the exchange from the corner of my eye, feeling like a Peeping Tom, even though the logical side of me knew Crystal could be his sister, a friend, a work acquaintance, or anyone other than the person I was assuming she was . . . his girlfriend.

But work acquaintances and friends usually didn't tell a guy they missed them, although it was possible the message was from his sister. *If he even has a sister.* But even most sisters didn't tell their brothers they missed them and wanted to know when they would call.

My shoulders sagged, and the salty bacon suddenly tasted rancid. The urge to push my food away took over, but I swallowed the mouthful I'd been chewing.

Are you seriously surprised he has a girlfriend? The guy's hot enough to be an underwear model.

Berating myself, I forced myself to finish eating and resolved to forget that Logan Smith was a potential mate.

Just as we finished breakfast, the sound of a vehicle driving up the road reached my ears, which only meant one thing. *My show's about to start.* Any lingering thoughts of Logan and his girlfriend disappeared.

Mike checked his watch. "Sounds like your first client's arriving. They're a little early, though."

Logan checked the time too. "They're definitely early."

My heart pounded as I wiped my mouth and stood. I picked up my lawn chair and hastily stowed it in the under-bus storage as Cecile and Mike grabbed the dishes before hurrying them into the bus. Logan stood with his hands on his hips, watching the distant driveway. I couldn't see the vehicle yet.

A moment later, Cecile bustled down the stairs and to my side. "Let's get to work. We'll have to do the dishes later."

Sunshine streamed across the wheat field swaying around us as we waited for my client. My heart rate picked up. Despite the fact that I'd done thousands of shows, butterflies still fluttered in my stomach at how grueling the coming sessions would be. Twenty-two clients guaranteed an exhausting day.

Logan frowned when he caught my expression, and his unique scent drifted my way. Closing my eyes, I inhaled it.

Surprisingly, my heartbeat slowed.

"No one is allowed near Daria until I've searched them." Logan moved closer to me, until his arm almost brushed mine. In jeans and a fitted T-shirt, he looked as sexy as hell.

Not that I'd noticed.

I gave him a stiff nod. "Of course. Not a problem."

Tension pulled along his limbs like a stretched rubber band ready to snap. Mike and Cecile hovered nervously at my side.

The rumble of the approaching vehicle grew louder until finally, it appeared. A pickup truck drove steadily along the gravel drive, the tall wheat brushing its sides.

I cocked my head when the driver's outline appeared. A large cowboy hat covered his head, and he sat straight and tall. Not something I would expect of an elderly client.

The man pulled up and hit the brakes, a cloud of dust rising. Rusty hinges squeaked when he opened the door and slid out.

Logan stepped in front of me. He did it so fast that all I could do was peek around his shoulder.

One thing was obvious from the young male swaggering toward us. He wasn't my client. My first client was supposed to be elderly.

So who is he?

"What can we do for you?" Logan reached one hand behind his back.

My eyes widened when his fingers slipped around a

handgun. Tucked into his jeans, the Glock was so well hidden that I hadn't seen it.

"Are you the ones who rented my granddad's barn for the day?" the man called.

I tentatively stepped out from behind Logan, getting a frown from my bodyguard.

Since the newcomer wore jeans, cowboy boots, and an old T-shirt, I guessed he worked with his granddad. Most likely, he was a farmer, perhaps even the one we'd seen working up the road. But the energy pouring off him made one thing perfectly clear—he wasn't happy we were here.

Mike shifted his weight from one foot to the other, and I caught his heavy sigh at the farmer's aggressive demeanor.

Better nip this in the bud.

I ginned brightly. "Morning, and yep, we're the ones who rented your granddad's barn."

The farmer placed his hands on his hips, his scowl turning to an appreciative leer as his gaze moved up and down my frame. I stiffened as a soft, discontented growl came from Logan.

"We'll be gone by nightfall," I added when the farmer still didn't reply.

Unfortunately, it quickly became apparent *why* he remained quiet. He was too busy ogling me. His eyes passed over me a second time, lingering much longer than necessary on my breasts.

Logan's hands clenched into fists.

The farmer didn't appear much older than me, but the

suggestive curl of his lip made it obvious this wasn't his first rodeo.

"Just what exactly are y'all doing here?" he asked, his voice dipping.

Logan put his hands on his hips. "None of your business."

When the farmer's lip curled in a sardonic smile at my bodyguard, I hastily added, "We're having a family reunion. This was a central location for us, so it seemed to make the most sense to meet here." The lie slipped easily off my tongue, years of practice coming to my aide. He wasn't the first local who didn't want us around.

The farmer's appreciative leer returned when he shifted his attention back to me. "A family reunion. That sounds like a long day."

If you only knew.

He scratched his chin. "Well, if you get bored visiting with second cousins, I'll be working in the field just up the road." His gaze dipped down to my boobs again. "I'd be happy to show you around town. We've got a great bar with pool and darts."

I suppressed an eye roll and replied with mocking sweetness, "Thanks. I'll keep that in mind."

The farmer hopped back into his truck, and a plume of dust filled the air when he turned and gunned it back down the road.

Logan swung my way, a scowl on his face. "I hope you're not actually going to meet that guy."

I laughed. "Are you kidding? I wouldn't touch him with a ten-foot pole."

Some of the tension eased from Logan's shoulders, and his lips tilted up, but just as quickly as his smile appeared, it vanished. "Is that how most guys treat you?"

"No, just the jerks."

Another low growl came from Logan. "That's one word for them, although I don't know if I'd put it that nicely."

Mike chuckled. "Neither would I."

Logan flashed him a grin.

Cecile checked her watch and smoothed her hair. "It's only a few minutes until ten. Let's all get in the barn." She hurried toward the decrepit structure. "Your first client's due any minute."

"Speaking of which . . ." Mike straightened and tried to see over the tall wheat fields that surrounded the barn. "Here comes another vehicle."

Sure enough, a cloud of gravel dust filled the air at the end of the long drive.

"Right on time." Cecile propelled me toward the barn. "Are you ready?"

I nervously straightened my shirt. "As ready as I can be given the circumstances."

The barn doors creaked as Cecile and I pushed them open then banged closed behind us when we entered the old building. The scent of rotting wood and molding hay filled my nose despite the multiple candles burning in the large space.

As the car drew nearer, the sounds of its engine

increased. When it ground to a halt, slamming doors followed.

"Please state your names," Logan said in a loud voice.

Through the barn slats, vertical slits of light poured in. I could make out two people facing Logan and Mike.

"Is this where Daria Gresham is?" The woman's voice was old and weak sounding.

Most definitely a client.

"Yep, this is the place," Mike replied cheerfully.

"Your name?" Logan stepped closer to her.

"Martha Walters, and this is my son, Ronald."

"Stand here and spread your legs. I'll do a quick search, then you'll be allowed to see her." Logan's voice turned businesslike.

"Ohhh," the old woman replied hesitantly. "All right."

Her son didn't say anything, but he appeared to be complying. I had a feeling Logan's imposing build might have had something to do with that. My bodyguard resembled a Mack truck. Not really the kind of guy people would want to mess with.

"This way." Logan's deep voice carried in the wind. When he pushed the doors open, his gaze alighted on mine. With the sun on his back, his shoulders filled the doorway.

I swallowed the fluttery feeling that had nothing to do with performing.

"Right over here." Cecile ushered Martha and Ronald to the chairs set up beside me. Logan watched everything from the side, his alert gaze missing nothing.

I sat up straighter and smiled, reminding myself that a girlfriend waited at home for Logan.

Ronald held his mother's hand. From the thinning hair covering his head, I guessed him to be in his fifties. Glasses perched on his nose, and despite the warm weather, he wore a jacket.

Martha dropped onto the seat. "Oomph." A flash of pain crossed her features.

She was in her eighties and looked every bit of it. Deep wrinkles covered her face, and thin lips pressed against her dentures.

"You're in pain." I leaned forward and readily took her hand. Healing sessions were the only time I willingly touched anybody. Paper-thin, cool, and dry skin stretched across the back of her hand as my light seeped out like a wispy fog from the storage chest I buried it in. "Tell me where."

The old woman's watery eyes met mine. "I've been waiting so long to see you." She gripped me with surprising strength. "You're my last hope!"

My gaze softened as any thoughts of Logan drifted to the back of my mind. It was time to work. "Show me where it hurts."

The woman pressed her free hand to her abdomen. "The cancer started here. They said there's nothing else they can do, but I have to live until next year. I just have to!"

"My daughter's first child is due in February." Ronald cleared his throat. "She and my mom are very close, and more than anything, they both want her to meet her first great-grandchild."

I nodded as the energy began to swirl inside me. It built up, like a slowly growing fire starting from burning embers. I coaxed it to a flame. This was my purpose. Healing was what I was meant to do.

"Let me help you to the bed, and we'll begin."

I continued holding her hand despite the unrelenting jolts of energy that made my fingers tingle, and with Ronald's help, I had Martha lie down on the portable bed.

Cecile approached and quietly told Ronald what I was going to do. She emphasized several times that it was imperative he didn't intervene.

"Close your eyes, Martha," I instructed. A breeze shifted through the barn, causing the candles to flicker. "You may feel a hot sensation, as if you're being burned, but it won't hurt you. It will heal you."

Martha nodded tightly. Shallow breaths made her chest rise and fall.

I lifted my hands, but before I could begin, she grabbed ahold of me once more, her touch provoking my light. "I trust you. My mother told me about your kind. She said that your magical light is real and that your mother once healed her sister. I know you can help me."

At the mention of my mother, a sharp longing filled my chest. I blinked rapidly to keep the traitorous tears from forming. "I'm happy to hear that."

I squeezed her back before placing her hand at her side. "Now, close your eyes."

Hovering my palms over her body, I focused on my healing light.

I flung the lid on my internal storage chest wide open, and my light completely poured out before it wound up my belly and into my arms. It warmed my skin, telling me everything that was happening inside my client.

Sick black energy rotted her insides. The disease swirled up into my palms, making itself known. *The cancer is everywhere. She's right.*

I closed my eyes and moved my palms, shifting and swaying above her until my healing light told me exactly where every cancer cell hid.

"I'm going to start now. You may feel some discomfort."

Ronald shuffled his feet behind me. Cecile stood at his side. She would stop him if he tried to interfere. I needed absolute concentration to rid someone of an illness. If my concentration broke during the process, it was possible my client would leave exactly as they'd come.

"Just take deep breaths, nice and slow," I told her.

I called upon the firelight within me until it felt as though flames consumed my insides. Pain shot down my arms into my fingertips, but I ignored it. Pain came with the territory.

Sweat formed on my brow as I clamped my teeth tightly together. *So much disease. So much illness.*

Minutes passed. Time ticked slowly by. As the sickness extracted from Martha and flowed into me, my arms shook.

A growl sounded behind me. *Logan.*

A sharp "Shh!" came from Cecile.

Martha's body grew healthier as I worked my light into her and scaled out the cancer. When I was certain that every tumorous cell was extracted from her body, I dropped my hands and panted quietly.

Next, came the hard part. The black illness that had been eating Martha from the inside out was inside *me*. I could feel it. Disease poured into my organs, my blood, and every fiber of my being.

I called up my light again, coaxing the fire and making it grow until it swallowed the shadowy disease relentlessly. A burst of light shot from my fingertips when it finished.

"What the hell!" Ronald's yell sounded muffled in my eardrums.

Folding over, I placed my hands on the bed as shivers wracked my body. Martha still lay motionless, but her skin held a healthy glow, and a soft smile tugged at her lips.

"Daria's hurting," Logan said in a gruff voice. "Why isn't anyone helping her?"

"No, Logan! You must never intervene!" Cecile's voice rang with authority. "You could hurt Daria if you do."

I gripped the bed's edge tightly. Even though I had done healings hundreds, if not thousands, of times, it still left me feeling weak and nauseated each time.

One down. Twenty-one to go.

CHAPTER FIVE

Throughout the day, I felt Logan's hovering presence even though I did my best to only focus on my clients. As each client came and went, he watched me perform. Though he stood in the corner, not saying a word, I still felt his tense energy.

After my fourteenth client, a seven-year-old sickened with neuroblastoma, fatigue rolled through me in steady waves. But watching that child walk out of the barn, after he'd needed to be carried in by his father, made my aching muscles and sweat-drenched face worth it.

"Thank you," the mother said, grabbing my hand as the rest of her family retreated to their beat-up vehicle. Tears rolled down her cheeks as the sound of her son's laughter filled the air outside the barn. She shoved a crumpled fifty-dollar bill into my hand. "I want to pay you more. I wish I could pay you the world, but the hospital bills were so much. We lost our house, and—"

"It's all right," I cut in, patting her hand before pulling away. Sharp sparks rolled up my arms from the contact we'd shared. "This is enough." I held up the bill which Cecile quickly took and stashed with the rest of my payments. "And that," I nodded to the sound of her now healthy child outside, "is more payment than anything in the bank."

Fat tears fell from her eyes when she swallowed audibly. "God bless you," she whispered before hurrying after her family.

When I turned to grab my water bottle, my gaze met Logan's. He was watching me again, his expression unreadable. I took a swig of cool water and wiped the sweat from my forehead with the cloth Cecile held out to me.

"Who's next?" I asked her.

THE SUN CONTINUED to progress across the sky as my clients came and went. Evening had arrived when I finished with my eighteenth client, the sky a dusky purple. The candles, long burned down, left the scent of smoke amidst the lavender and moldy hay.

When the door closed behind my latest client, I collapsed onto one of the chairs, still panting from exertion. That case had been particularly brutal. Their genetic disease had been buried in every cell of their body, making extraction particularly hard.

Logan pushed away from the wall, advancing toward Cecile. "Shouldn't she take another break?" he asked under his breath. "She's so tired she can't even stand."

"I'm fine," I said, even though my hand shook when I reached for my water.

"You don't *look* fine." Logan handed me my water before I could retrieve it.

Cecile patted my forehead with the towel. "Logan's right. You do look tired, and you're quite pale. We can cancel the rest if need be."

Logan nodded, his watchful gaze assessing me again.

I took the towel from Cecile. "No. I'll do it."

Logan's mouth opened, but he closed it. However, that worried look crossed his features again. "Are you really going to keep going?"

"Of course. I'm used to working long days. Besides, I have tomorrow off. I'll sleep in."

"Why not just reschedule the rest?"

I took another drink of water. "It's not that easy. If I cancel, my remaining clients are out of luck since all of my days are fully booked. Any time I have to end a show early . . ." I paused, picturing the absolute despair that flashed through my clients' eyes. Those forlorn and hopeless looks left an aching hole in my chest. "Well, let's just say, I don't like letting them down."

"So you help them even though it hurts you."

"It doesn't hurt me for long. For the most part, it's just . . . exhausting."

Cecile rubbed my back. "Logan's right. You should take a break."

Her touch caused a shifting of energy beneath my skin, like water flowing under a bridge. She pulled away just before the sensation grew to something unbearable and checked her watch again. "We have a spare twenty minutes. How about you close your eyes for a bit?"

My next client had just called to say they had a flat tire and were running late. The anxiety in the woman's tone had flowed through the call, like electricity shooting along a power line. Cecile had assured her we would still proceed, but she would have to wait until the end of the night.

"So if client nineteen is running late, who's client twenty?" I forced myself to sit up straighter, more for Logan's benefit than mine. A deep groove had settled between his eyes.

Cecile glanced at the schedule on her clipboard. "A forty-year-old female named Lucy Basig, recently diagnosed with pancreatic cancer. Stage four. Her doctors have given her a few months to live."

"So it won't be an easy one." Cancer that advanced always took extra effort.

Logan made a discontented sound as faint banging noises came from the bus.

"Sounds like Mike has woken up," I said, trying to distract Logan.

He didn't give the bus a glance.

I was about to lean back in the chair and close my eyes when the sound of a car driving up the gravel drive had me sitting up straighter. "Is Lucy already here?"

Cecile set her clipboard down. "She shouldn't be. I gave them strict instructions to not arrive until her designated time and explained how we never like people waiting at the door."

"I'll check it out." Logan strode out the barn door, a strong gust of wind following in his wake.

My long blond hair fluttered across my cheeks.

Cecile checked her watch again. "It's only 8:10. That would make them twenty minutes early."

Flashing red and blue lights penetrated the barn's slats. Cecile's frown grew. "That looks like a police car."

"Police?" My insides chilled. The haunting words from my mother rose in my mind. *"Always avoid the police. They like to trick us, make us think we can trust them, but we can't. My grandmother made that mistake once. She was committed to a mental institution. For months, she never saw the light of day."*

The flashing lights swirled around, and the police cruiser rolled to a stop outside. Slamming car doors followed.

"What can we do for you?" Logan called as Cecile and I crept closer to the barn door to listen.

"We got a call. Said there's been a lot of unusual traffic to the area, and folks are worried about disturbing the peace," the officer replied. He sounded young and assertive.

I rolled my eyes. *Great. Just what we need.* Rookie officers were the worst, as if they were on a mission to prove themselves and show the world they were in charge.

But the next voice I heard set my teeth on edge. "I knew something wasn't right when I stopped by earlier." The young farmer, the one who'd so graciously offered to show me around his small town, had returned.

I gritted my teeth and slipped through the barn doors, Cecile hot on my heels.

The sun was setting. Hazy purple clouds filled the western sky, and a few stars appeared, but there was enough light from the glaring police cruiser headlights to see everyone's faces clearly.

The young officer's eyes narrowed when I approached.

"Officer, what can we do for you?" I asked sweetly, yet annoyance dripped in my tone. I glared at the farmer.

Logan stiffened and stepped closer to my side.

The officer nodded toward Logan. "As I was telling this man, we've had calls about disturbances in the area. A lot of traffic has been seen coming up and down this road today. That's unusual for these parts."

Cecile's smile tightened. "We have all of the necessary papers for conducting business here. I can get them—"

"Business?" The farmer put his hands on his hips. "I thought you were having a family reunion? Why would you need business papers for that?"

Cecile cast me a pained look.

I mouthed that it was okay. Since our cover was blown, there was no point trying to hide anything anymore.

"I'm here seeing clients," I replied to the officer,

ignoring the farmer. "That's why there has been so much traffic."

"And as I was saying," Cecile added, "I have the necessary documents for the business we're conducting here."

The officer cocked his head, looking genuinely perplexed. "Just what kind of business are you doing?"

A bang came from the bus door when Mike emerged, stuffing his shirt into his pants as he jogged our way. Wet, dark ringlets of hair fell on his shoulders, his bushy mustache smooth. From the looks of it, he'd just showered and dressed, once again ready to drive us through the night.

"I have the papers right here!" He waved them in the air.

Logan remained quiet, but his gaze continually swiveled around, and given the tense way he stood, he was ready to jump into action if needed.

The officer took the papers from Mike and snapped his flashlight on. Bright light flowed across the forms. The farmer stepped closer and peered over the officer's shoulder.

A gust of wind shot across the fields, and I pushed my hair back. I bit my lip, eyeing the sky.

More stars were emerging. It was getting darker by the second, and who knew how much longer we had before my next client arrived. Once they did, I would need to get back to work.

"So what exactly do you do?" the officer asked as he scanned the papers.

"I'm a supernatural healer. I travel around the country

and heal those who are seriously ill. I'm here today seeing clients."

Both the officer and farmer glanced up.

The officer's eyebrows rose. "A supernatural . . . what?"

"A healer." Cecile took the papers back. "Daria is a very sought-after healer by those who are gravely ill. She's well renowned for what she does."

"Is that right?" the officer replied skeptically and snapped his flashlight off.

I crossed my arms defensively. I knew what was coming.

"Are you doing witchcraft or something?" The farmer's eyes narrowed, and he took a step closer to me. "My granddad never approved any séances out here or said it was okay to be practicing any voodoo shit."

Logan moved closer to me when I replied through gritted teeth, "It's not séances, and it's not voodoo."

A car engine rumbled in the distance. In the twilight, a hazy cloud of gravel dust rose from the end of the drive like mist from a moor.

Logan's attention shifted to the new vehicle. My next client had arrived.

"So?" the farmer demanded. "Is that what you're doing out here?" He sidestepped Logan so he could see me better. The flirtatious, leering expression he'd worn earlier in the day had been replaced with one of revulsion and something darker.

Hate.

Logan tensed again, his attention waffling between the

farmer and the new vehicle approaching, as if trying to deduce which posed the greater threat. After all, we thought the car arriving held my next client, but maybe it didn't.

I jutted my chin up. "What I'm doing is healing people. You can call that whatever you like."

The police officer sighed and holstered his flashlight. "Well, whatever she's doing, the paperwork is legal. Not much I can do about that." From his regretful tone, he also seemed to share the farmer's revulsion.

"Well, there's something *I* can do," the farmer said. He stepped closer to me.

Logan immediately shielded my body with his and widened his stance, but it didn't stop the farmer's aggression.

"You get off our land!" the farmer yelled. Veins bulged in his neck as spittle flew from his mouth. "We don't want your kind around here!"

My kind? I couldn't believe I was still hearing things like that in the twenty-first century. I peered around Logan and leveled the farmer with an icy stare. "I believe we signed a deal with your grandfather. Not you."

The approaching car's engine grew louder, and everyone turned as an old Buick pulled into the clearing. The outlines of two people sat in the cab.

Nighttime had fully set in, bringing with it the sound of crickets and rodents scurrying in the field. Mike's chest rose and fell heavily. He cast Cecile an anxious look.

"Even if you're conducting legitimate business, you still

need the landowner's permission to be here," the officer cut in.

"He gave us permission," Cecile replied.

A woman stepped out of the Buick's passenger door. She fit the description of my next client, Lucy Basig. Limping, she rounded the Buick's hood.

In the cruiser's bright headlights, she looked thin and frail. The man I assumed was her husband hurried around the hood to support her. She draped a bird-like arm around his shoulders and sagged like a wilted flower.

They both looked middle-aged, except he appeared healthy. Strong shoulders and a flat abdomen pressed against his T-shirt. It was obvious he worked out.

"Is this where we meet Daria Gresham?" he asked warily, his gaze darting between the officer, the farmer, and me.

"No. Miss Gresham," the farmer replied, sneering at my name, "was just leaving."

"But your grandfather said I could—"

The officer held up his hand. "I know Earl quite well. Our families go way back, and I can assure you he wouldn't want a *supernatural healer* doing business on his land. Josh here tells me he thought you all were having a family reunion."

"But we paid!" Cecile said hotly.

"The way I see it, you've been here all day, so your time is done." The young officer turned to the farmer. "Don't you agree, Josh?"

Josh smirked at the officer as anger rose in me swiftly

and strongly. They obviously knew one another. They probably grew up together or were old high school buddies. Whatever the case, Josh had the law on his side, which only meant one thing.

We were being kicked out, and my remaining clients would not be seen.

CHAPTER SIX

"But you have to see her!" Lucy's husband yelled from outside the barn.

Logan stayed near my side as the officer and Josh stood watch while we packed up. However, my client's husband showed no signs of leaving. He stood in the barn doorway, his wife still hanging from his arm, looking entirely exhausted.

"I'm sorry," Cecile replied. "But given the circumstances, that is now impossible." She flashed a dark look toward the farmer and the officer before trying to usher Lucy and her husband back to their car.

But he held his ground. "We just drove seven hours to see her! And we already paid. Not to mention we've been waiting for months for this. Daria is our last hope!" The man ground his teeth together so hard I thought his jaw would snap.

My hands shook as I packed the remaining candles. I

wanted to go to Lucy and her husband, to reassure them that I could see them at my next show in two days, even though it would be another long drive for them, but years of disappointing people had instilled several cold hard facts into my life: one, being able to help someone was never a guarantee no matter how much I wanted to, and two, if I went to them now it would only make the situation worse. I'd learned that the hard way.

"I'm sorry." Cecile placed her hand firmly on the man's arm and steered him away, while Logan watched him closely as though assessing to see if he'd turn violent. "Without a calm, peaceful environment, Daria is unable to work. You can speak to the officer and the farmer out there about that. Daria would happily see you now, if she were able to."

The husband turned, shifting his anger to the two outside. He stalked out, dragging Lucy with him.

I shut my eyes tightly when he began yelling.

Even after years of such encounters, I still shook every time they happened. Lucy, whose sick body dangled from her husband's firm grasp, had counted on me. Her husband had trusted me. They'd driven hundreds of miles to have her cured, and I'd promised to help them.

But Cecile was right. Without a quiet environment devoid of distractions, I couldn't help them. I needed absolute peace and silence to work my gift.

The only option we had was to treat her on the bus while we drove away, and that *wasn't* an option. The jostles and dips of a moving vehicle proved too hazardous to my sick client and me.

And even if Lucy and her husband offered to buy a hotel room and have me treat her there, I couldn't. Once word got out that I would help someone under any circumstances, I would never live in peace. People would hunt me down to demand I cure them. It wouldn't just be a crazy stalker I ran from. It would be everyone.

My mother had taught me that. While our gift was created to help others, we also needed to protect ourselves. The Gresham women walked a fine line.

"You can't make us leave! You just can't!" the husband yelled.

"Get in your vehicle now, sir!" the police officer replied. "I'm not asking!"

Finally, Lucy and her husband slid into their car, the husband continuing to yell at the officer.

Somehow Mike, Logan, and I kept packing our supplies as Cecile slipped back into the barn. She raised a shaky hand to tuck the wispy strands of hair into her bun.

"I've already contacted the remaining three clients and told them our work location has been compromised." She bustled to the portable bed, the last thing to pack. "I told them we'll do our best to work them into your schedule if possible, and I managed to slip Lucy instructions for how to find your next venue. It will be up to them to try to make it. Now, let's finish up here and get going."

Logan's commanding presence hovered behind me, like an impending storm about to let loose.

"Are you okay?" His quiet question, laced with concern, made my head snap up.

I nodded. "Yeah. I'm fine."

"You don't *look* fine."

"Well . . . unfortunately, things like this come with the territory."

His eyebrows knitted.

"Let's get everything on the bus and go." I reached for the box of supplies, but he intercepted.

"I'll carry it. Just follow me and stay behind me."

"You done in here?" Josh's sharp question filled the air when he poked his head into the barn.

His nasal tone made me grimace.

"We're leaving now," Mike called, his usual cheerful demeanor absent. He hoisted the chairs under his arms while Logan grabbed the bed and stacked the box he'd been carrying on top of it.

Despite Logan's protests that I not carry anything, I grabbed the last of the supplies before following him out. Cecile gave the barn a once-over and closed the doors behind us. We left the barn exactly as we'd found it.

The sliver of a crescent moon shone as soft rustling from the wheat stalks swayed in the breeze. A million stars grazed the sky.

None of us said a thing as we packed the bus, but Josh's sneer was impossible to ignore, and the cold way the officer watched me sent chills down my spine. I'd experienced hate before. That was something all Gresham women understood, but it never made it any easier.

"We'll follow you out, just to make sure you reach the highway." The officer strode to his police cruiser as Josh spat in the grass.

"We'll be fine. No need for an escort," Mike replied. He jumped onto the bus and started the engine. The loud rumble made the ground vibrate.

Cecile and I climbed the stairs next and Logan followed. An undercurrent of anger shimmered around my bodyguard. Darting an angry glare at the officer and Josh, Logan placed his hand on my lower back and guided me farther into the bus, not knowing that any touch normally triggered my light.

At the subtle contact, desire zinged inside my abdomen, taking me completely by surprise, especially considering how tired I was. My eyes widened, and I hastily inched forward until his hand dropped.

"You head on to bed, Dar." Mike closed the bus door, a hiss emitting from the mechanics before he shifted into reverse. The bus lurched. "I'll drive us to a rest stop for the night so we can all get some decent sleep."

Cecile fussed around me by the couches while Logan stood at my side.

"Why don't you change into your pajamas, honey. You look dead on your feet." Cecile smoothed my hair. "In thirty minutes, those two will be long gone." She glared out the window at the officer and Josh.

"I'm okay, Cece. How about you touch base with the clients again and see if you can work them more firmly into my schedule later this week. I'm sure they're all disappointed."

Cecile finished tucking a stray strand of hair behind my ear before she nodded. "All right. I'll see what I can do."

She retreated to the front of the bus as Mike drove us down the gravel driveway. Behind us came the sounds of another vehicle. The officer and Josh were following us despite our protests that it wasn't needed. Most likely, they would see us to the county line, just to ensure we left.

Logan trailed behind me to the bunks, not saying anything. His gaze followed me as I grabbed my night-clothes off my bed, my movements heavy as exhaustion set in.

The bus continued to vibrate under my soles. Acutely aware of Logan's presence and my growing response to his touch, I swallowed sharply. I glanced up at him through my lashes. "You've done enough for today. You should turn in, too, unless there's something else you need to do."

Logan's brow furrowed. "I'd feel better knowing that we're far away from those ignorant pricks who harassed you tonight. From the sounds of it, they're still following us."

"Honestly, there's not much any of us can do about that."

He cocked his head. "Is that something you deal with a lot? Do people often harass you?"

I nodded. The soft worn cotton of my pajamas felt familiar beneath my fingertips. "It happens often enough that we know how to deal with it."

"I didn't know that."

Though I tried to smile, the fatigue that rolled through me made it difficult. "Someone wants to kill me. It shouldn't be that surprising, but it's fine. Really, it is. My mom and my nan had to deal with the same sort of harassment as did all of my ancestors. It's something my family is used to. Throughout the centuries, we've adapted as needed."

Logan's jaw locked before he said quietly, "It doesn't have to be that way."

I cocked my head, not entirely sure what he meant by that.

Logan remained quiet, his gaze staying on me. A deep swirling emotion swam behind his dark irises.

I had no idea what he was thinking, and I had to remind myself again that I was his boss, and that the tightening in my stomach was an entirely unprofessional reaction to him. Because at the moment, I wanted nothing more than to drown in those stormy eyes.

I abruptly twirled away and removed my earrings with shaky fingers. Despite trying to control my reaction, my hands continued to tremble when I placed my earrings in the jewelry box by my bunk.

We reached an intersection in the county road, and Mike turned us onto the highway. From the sounds of it, Josh and the cop were still following.

Logan reached a hand up to steady himself when the bus tilted. "Your show today was—" That groove appeared between his eyes again. "I guess I've never seen anyone so devoted to helping others. Not like you are. Have you always drained yourself mentally to heal other people?"

I shrugged and fiddled with my pajamas. "Well, yes. It's part of my job. Healing people doesn't come without consequences."

"Yet the consequences are all yours, not theirs, and you still choose to do it."

"It's either that or they stay sick."

His eyebrows knitted more. "Many would leave them to die. You haven't chosen an easy profession."

A tired smile curved my lips up. "This job chose me. I'm a Gresham. This is what I was born to do. I can't run from that." I shifted from one foot to the other. Since Logan's hand still gripped the edge of my bed, he stood so close. If I leaned a few inches to the right, my cheek would brush his arm.

I abruptly straightened. "I'd better get to bed."

Logan cleared his throat and took a step back. "Yeah, of course. I didn't mean to hold you up."

He was halfway to the front of the bus before a response formed on my lips.

CHAPTER SEVEN

Quiet voices woke me the next day. I opened my eyes, expecting to see Logan asleep across the aisle as Cecile and Mike spoke in the front, but all that greeted me was an empty bed with tangled sheets.

Gurgling from the coffee pot reached my ears. The tantalizing fragrance and familiar sound told me a new pot was brewing.

After a quick peek at the bunks below, it became apparent everybody else was up. Bright sunlight peeked through the curtained windows. *I definitely missed breakfast.* But at least I felt rested.

The rumbling bus engine and swaying old suspension system were absent. Since we were parked, I figured we'd made it to the rest stop.

Staying in my bunk, I listened to the conversation

taking place only yards away. Everyone's voices were hushed as they tried to not wake me.

"I promised I would tell her." Logan's tone, while soft, held a hint of irritation.

Mike's reply came readily. "This is going to scare the crap out of her. We can't tell her."

"Mike's right," Cecile whispered. "The previous emails frightened her enough. This one may send her over the edge."

My heart rate increased. Obviously, I'd received a new message from my stalker, apparently worse than the previous ones.

"I don't know," Logan grumbled. His movements sounded restless, as if he were pacing. "I promised to tell her."

"You can't!" Cecile hissed.

I hopped off my bed and landed with a quiet thump.

The conversation stopped, and Logan whirled around to face me. Mussed dark hair stood up on his head, as if he'd been running his fingers through it.

I padded to the three of them. "What will scare the crap out of me?"

Mike and Cecile shared guilty looks from where they sat on the couch. Logan simply raked a hand through his hair.

Cecile fingered her bun. That telltale sign gave her away. "Oh . . . um . . . we didn't realize you were awake, Dar." A strained smile stretched across her face.

I frowned and put my hands on my hips. "I heard you all talking. What are you keeping from me?"

Mike threw up his hands. "Okay. We're caught! The psycho sent a new email last night, but it seems he's added a new twist to his messages. He's no longer just threatening your life."

I gulped, and shallow breaths filled my chest. "What do you mean?"

Logan handed me my laptop. My email was open.

Dear Ms. Gresham,

I'm disappointed that you haven't replied to my messages. I know that you're getting them. It only makes me itch to kill you.

However, considering I'm a fair person, I've decided to make a deal with you. I won't end your life if you agree to pay me fifty thousand dollars.

Tick tock. Tick tock. Your time is running out, witch. I hope you make the right choice.

Your biggest fan.

A stone settled in my stomach and became heavier and heavier with each sentence I read as if weighing me down and pushing me to the floor. By the time I finished reading, I dropped onto the couch by Mike.

"That's extortion!"

Logan nodded. "Exactly."

I reread the email more slowly.

Bile rose in my throat. My hands were gripping the

laptop so tightly that Logan had to pry it away. He snapped it closed and set it aside.

"He's making even more threats now, Daria," Cecile said. "We should really go to the police."

Tangled snarls threaded through my fingers when I tried to run a hand through my hair. I bit my lip before shaking my head vigorously. "You saw what the police were like yesterday. You know firsthand how they treat me. I can't go to them. I won't forget what my mother taught me."

"But this is serious, Dar." Cecile moved from her seat to sit beside me. "Your own mother would probably have had second thoughts about contacting the police by now. You need to think about your safety. Even if this bastard is full of hot air and wouldn't actually do anything, he's now trying to steal money from you. Money you don't have."

I waited for Logan to chime in, also agreeing that we should contact the police, but surprisingly, he stayed quiet.

Mike scooted closer to my other side, sandwiching me between him and Cecile. "She's right, Dar. We're getting in over our heads. We should call the cops."

He and Cecile loomed around me, creating a wall of opposition as my gift sparked to life, their close presence lighting up my nerves.

I abruptly stood, breaking the contact. "No. Not yet. I'm not ready to do that."

Before either of them could respond, I raced to the bathroom, my feet thumping against the floor.

Slamming the door behind me, I crumpled in a heap.

The hollow door pressed against my back as my butt landed hard on the faded linoleum of the cramped space. I drew my knees up and buried my head in my hands.

Though the sick bastard was demanding money, the police weren't the right answer. Mike and Cecile *knew* what my family and I had gone through with law enforcement. No way was I going to the police.

Tears pooled in my eyes. More than ever, I wished my mom and my nan were with me. They would know what to do, and they would be on my side. They'd *always* been on my side. Together, we would have figured a way out. *I miss you, guys. I miss you so much!*

A soft knock came at the door. "Daria?" Logan's deep voice carried through the flimsy material.

Hastily, I scrambled to my feet. The image that stared back at me in the mirror was that of a blotchy face and wild hair.

"Just a minute!"

I splashed cold water on my face and patted my cheeks dry. Pink skin still rimmed my turquoise eyes, but I pushed my emotions down. One of my small bags sat on the floor. I'd stashed it in the bathroom the previous day after my embarrassing encounter with Logan in which I'd worn only a towel.

After rummaging through it, I found a pair of cut-off jean shorts, a simple T-shirt, and, hallelujah, a bra. I threw them on as several hard, cold facts settled in my mind.

My mom and my nan were dead and weren't coming back. I was on my own, but I wouldn't forget what my mother had taught me. I was a Gresham. We'd been perse-cuted for centuries. What I was facing, all of my ancestors had dealt with at some point in their lives. *I won't succumb to this creep, and I won't let him beat me.*

"Daria, *please* open the door."

Grasping the door handle, I debated my options. I wanted to trust Logan, to open the door and know he would never hide anything from me again, but I hesitated. Leaning my head against the door, I replied through the hollow material, "You told me you would tell me if he emailed."

A soft thud came from the other side, as though he'd just rested his forehead against the door too. "I was going to show it to you, really. I didn't want to keep it from you, but Cecile and Mike were adamant you not see it."

"They're always trying to protect me, but hiding things from me isn't the answer." I ran my hand over the smooth door handle.

A long silence followed before he said quietly, "I should have told you right away. Please believe me when I say that you can trust me." Several moments passed. "Will you open the door now?"

The ache in his voice was my undoing. I finally opened the door.

Logan's large frame dominated the space. His gaze swept over me. "You're dressed."

"I stashed some clothes in here after . . ." My cheeks heated.

As he stepped closer, his lips quirked up. "Are you okay?"

"Yeah, I'm fine, but I don't want to go to the police. I really don't."

"Don't worry. I don't think the police are necessary."

I cocked my head and opened my mouth to ask why, but he turned.

"How about we go up front and have a seat. Then we can talk about everything." He turned, and I followed while trying to figure out why he wouldn't go to the police.

"Do you want a cup of coffee?" Logan asked when we passed the kitchen.

"Yeah, sure."

He stopped to pour us both cups, but I stepped past him and plopped down on the couch, the ancient cushion sinking like the *Titanic*. After a quick glance around the bus, I realized Cecile and Mike were gone. I pulled back the curtains on the window.

A typical rest stop loomed outside: a large brick building with pamphlets and flyers lining the plastic cubbies hooked to the exterior, a green grassy lawn, and a small playground. Rolling brown hills covered in dry grass filled the landscape behind it.

"Do you know where they went?" I asked when Logan approached with two cups of steaming coffee. The scent made my mouth water. Letting the curtain fall back into place, I wrapped my fingers around the mug he handed to me.

"Inside the rest stop. Both wanted to shower, and I think they could tell you wanted some space."

I grimaced. "Was it the slamming door that gave it away?"

He smiled again, his perfect white teeth flashing. "Perhaps."

Logan leaned against the wall and brought his cup to his lips. He wore another dark T-shirt and jeans. The ensemble seemed his wardrobe of choice. The thin cotton material stretched across his broad shoulders and strong chest. Defined pectoral muscles pressed against the fabric like granite blocks.

I hastily looked away and took a sip of coffee. "So, are you going to tell me why you don't think we need the police?"

Logan scratched his jaw, his fingers running over the stubble. "Remember my friend I told you about? The one good with computers?"

I perked up. "Yeah, have you heard from him?"

"Just did this morning. He's free now, so he's going to look into those emails."

I took another sip of coffee. "And you think he can figure out where my stalker is?"

"If anybody can, it's him."

"But that still doesn't explain why you don't think we need the police. Don't get me wrong, I'm glad you don't, but I have to admit . . . I'm a little surprised."

"I have a few other friends who may be able to help. I

think we can handle what's going on here without involving the cops."

Shifting, I drew my feet beneath me. "Okay, now I'm really intrigued. Are your friends like, private investigators or something?"

He looked away as he took another sip of coffee. "Something like that."

Logan's evasive answers only made my curiosity grow, but I shifted my attention to the window. "Where are we?"

"The eastern edge of Wyoming."

Since it was my day off, the entire afternoon stretched ahead. My gaze drifted to the rolling hills behind the rest stop. The thought of fresh air filling my lungs had me draining my coffee and setting it down.

"I think I'm going to go for a walk. I won't be gone long." I scribbled a quick note to Cecile and Mike, letting them know my plans.

Logan set his cup beside mine. It was still half full. "I'll come with you."

He then grabbed his handgun, which he stored near the front of the bus. My eyes bulged when he tucked it into his waistband.

I almost replied that his company wasn't necessary, but then I remembered I'd hired him to do just that. And while I doubted my stalker was near, in reality, he could be. After all, we had no idea who he was, and even more frightening, we had no idea *where* he was.

CHAPTER EIGHT

Hiking trails cut through the hills behind the rest stop. A quick glance at the trailhead sign revealed several miles of tracks.

The rest stop wasn't busy. Only a few other vehicles filled the lot, but everyone seemed to be stopping only to use the restroom or the shower facilities before hopping back in their vehicles and taking off again. Nobody hiked the distant hills.

A breeze lifted my hair as I studied the map. The Rockies loomed just west of us, their snowy peaks brushing the sky. The scent of milkweed hung in the air as I trailed my finger over the worn material.

"This one looks all right." I pointed at a looping trail that was just over four miles.

Logan leaned closer. Out in the sunshine, his dark hair shone like silk while it whipped around his ears. "That one's fine, but it looks the steepest. Is that what you want?"

I shrugged. "I try to exercise when I can, but obviously, it's hard with our lifestyle."

"And you're not too tired from your show last night?"

"Nope. I slept well, and I feel fine."

He gestured toward the trail. "Then lead the way."

I paused to twirl my hair up into a ponytail. I had to lean backward, arching my back, since the wind made it hard. Logan abruptly lifted his gaze over my head. I flushed. The arching movement had made my breasts strain against my shirt.

When I finally had my hair under control, I relaxed my posture, but my cheeks still heated. My damn boobs had again demanded attention, and from the stiff way Logan stood, he'd apparently noticed, although he'd once again acted like a gentleman.

"Ready?" I asked.

He smiled, but it appeared strained. "Whenever you are."

I took off from the trailhead at a brisk walk, my feet kicking up the dry earth. Wind brushed against my bare arms and legs. My embarrassment quickly evaporated as the clean air cleansed my soul.

We didn't talk as we walked, but I could feel Logan behind me. Despite the vigorous pace, he never sounded winded. I barely heard his breathing, but his presence was tangible. His energy flowed over me like a hot caress.

Tiny pebbles in the dirt brushed against the soles of my shoes as the miles disappeared behind us. The trail turned upward and grew steeper the farther we went, the pungent scent of yarrow filling the breeze. The tiny white wild-flowers dotted the landscape.

Ahead, the steep hill's peak loomed. Only a dozen yards stood between me and the top. My breath exhaled in harsh pants as I struggled to reach the summit.

I was almost at the precipice when a smile broke across my face. *Just about there!*

A few small trees grew up from the brush. I grabbed a branch, high-stepping onto a rock.

"Daria! Watch out!" Logan called.

A rattle cut through the wind. My eyes widened when I spotted a huge rattlesnake coiled on the rock, only inches from my foot.

I shrieked and pushed away so hard I fell backward. Though I flung my arms out to steady myself, it was no use. I'd been going too fast and pushed back too hard. The sky appeared above as I fell alarmingly fast.

Just when I expected my head to hit the ground, a large arm wrapped around my waist, stopping my fall and pulling me upright. Logan's other hand gripped a large boulder, steadying us.

"Holy crap!" I exclaimed. "Did you see how big that snake was?"

Logan's granite chest pressed into my back as I slid down his body. The movement made his arm inch up higher until it was hooked around my ribcage, just beneath my breasts. The weight of my boobs rested on his forearm. My heart pounded harder, my fear over the snake disappearing as something else commanded my attention.

Logan cleared his throat. "Yeah, I did, but it's already slithering away. See?"

I caught a glimpse of the rattler's tail disappearing into the tall grass, and I shuddered, realizing how closely I'd come to being bitten, but that awareness didn't stop the feel of Logan's body pressed so intimately against mine. Fireworks shot off in my blood. Once again, my light didn't stir. Instead, tingles of desire coursed through my veins.

Logan's entire body grew rigid.

I panted quietly. Neither of us moved.

"Sorry," I finally managed. "For freaking out. Thanks for catching me."

"No worries. I'll . . . um . . ." His arm was still around me. "Are you hurt? It didn't bite you, right?"

"Nope. I'm totally fine."

"Right. I mean, good." He let go. In the process, his arm brushed against my breasts, causing the heat in my core to grow.

Cool wind suddenly washed over my back. Logan stood a yard away, having moved incredibly fast.

Trying to appear casual, I smoothed back my hair, but Logan's scent wasn't helping. It swam through my senses like a drug, making my head spin. It took at least a few seconds before my feet felt firmly anchored on the earth. *Why does he have to smell so good?* His sandalwood scent, tinged with a hint of sweat made tingles race down my spine.

When I turned to face him, his eyes were closed. A muscle in his jaw ticked.

I took a deep breath and eyed the hill's peak, a bit more warily since I knew snakes lingered around the rocks. "Should we get going?"

Logan's eyes opened. His pupils were dilated and had a faint glow. I narrowed my gaze, stepping closer to him. He blinked, and the glow disappeared.

What the hell?

He stood up straighter, his body rigid. "Yeah. I'll follow you. Just try to be more careful this time. Snakes love rocks."

I mentally berated myself. I knew rattlers lived in the west, and I did enough hiking to know I needed to be mindful of them, but having a six-foot-three mountain of a man following me on a hike proved more distracting than I'd appreciated.

Straightening my shoulders, I climbed up the remaining path, being cautious with where I put my hands and feet. Thankfully, the lone snake had disappeared and no others lingered.

A moment later, I stood on the top. The wind whipped even stronger up here, making my ponytail slap against my face.

Logan effortlessly jogged up the last few feet of trail, as if hiking up a mountainous slope were no different from ambling along a city street.

Crossing my arms, I gazed down at the trail we'd just climbed, trying to act indifferent even though the physical contact I'd just shared with Logan still made my heart pound. The steep hillside swept out in front of us. The rest stop and parking lot were visible in the distance, our bus and a lone car parked in the lot.

"Should we head back?" I peeked up at him.

He shrugged. "It's your day off, right? Are you in a hurry to get back?"

I cocked my head as the wind blew. "No. I guess not."

"We might as well enjoy the view." He surveyed the flat ground, probably making sure no other snakes occupied the area before sitting down.

He leaned back on his forearms casually. Obviously, one of us had fully recovered from the feel of our bodies touching. *Yeah, cause the dude has a girlfriend.*

I shaded my eyes and looked for a good place to sit. After spotting a patch of dry grass a yard away—snake free —I sank to the ground and crossed my legs, thankful that the patchy grass kept me a safe distance from Logan so I couldn't accidentally touch him.

The wind drifted around us as the sun warmed my skin.

I closed my eyes and tilted my chin up. The silence between us, the strong breeze, and the sweet scent of grass helped slow my pounding heart.

"This is nice," I finally said. "I can't remember the last time I spent time outside like this."

The sound of Logan shifting had my eyes opening. He had stretched out on his side, his head cupped in his hand.

His long fingers threaded through his thick hair, and his thighs looked chiseled through his worn jeans.

I quickly averted my gaze and plucked a piece of grass.

When neither of us said anything more, I asked awkwardly, "So . . . where are you from?" The fact that I didn't know much about my bodyguard struck me. In the forty-eight hours we'd known each other, I'd learned a few things: he was honest and incredibly protective—which was a no-brainer given his job—he probably had a girlfriend, and apparently, his friends came with mad computer skills. But all in all, that was the extent of what I knew about Logan Smith.

"Originally?" He glanced my way as he picked up a pebble with his free hand and threw it. The small rock sailed through the air so far that I couldn't tell where it landed. "I grew up here, in Wyoming, but now I live in Idaho."

I played with the grass between my fingers. "Is your family still here?"

"Yeah, my parents have been in the same spot for thirty years. My younger sister—she's only sixteen—still lives at home with them, but my brother lives on his own in town."

I perked up when I heard he had a sister, but I didn't want to sound too desperate for information on her.

"So how old's your brother?"

"Twenty-three, two years younger than me."

"And what are their names?"

"Lila and Lucas."

So not Crystal. My shoulders slumped. Any lingering

hope I had that Logan didn't have a girlfriend disappeared like light in a black hole. *Well, that's settled then. He and I will just be work associates despite him being a potential mate.*

Logan picked up another pebble before adding, "My other brothers are with me in Idaho."

I shoved my disappointment away. "How many brothers do you have?"

He shifted his gaze, cutting eye contact. "Well . . . they're not blood brothers, but there are a few guys in my life I consider brothers."

"From the military?"

He threw the rock. "You could say that."

I frowned, not entirely sure what he meant by that. "Are these the friends you were talking about back at the bus?"

"Yep, same ones."

"And that's why you don't think we need the police? Your friends have ties to the military, so they're . . . what? Good with weapons? Dealing with bad guys?"

A crooked smile lifted the corner of his mouth. "Something like that." He glanced my way, squinting in the bright sunlight. "And what about you? Where did you grow up?"

Okay, point taken. Logan didn't want to divulge details about his friends.

I shrugged it off, even though I felt as curious as a cat. I waved toward the bus in the distant parking lot. "You're looking at it."

"In that bus?"

"More or less. My mom and I—" My chest tightened at the thought of my mother. I cleared my throat. "My mom and I grew up touring the US and part of Canada with my nan. As supernatural healers, our livelihood meant we moved constantly."

"Have you always lived on a bus?"

"Pretty much. We never owned a house, although if we stayed anywhere for more than a few months, we'd rent an apartment, but for the most part, I grew up in a tour bus. We bought that one about fifteen years ago."

Logan's head cocked. "Instead of traveling, why not open a clinic and stay put somewhere? It seems like it would be easier to have people come to you."

I winced. "We tried that. Well, not me but my mom and my nan did before I was born, but it didn't work. Either they were harassed by locals since what they did was taboo, or sick people would show up and refuse to leave until they'd been healed. The lines never stopped, and my mom said they couldn't keep up. It was too exhausting, and their work never ended." I ran my hand over the dry grass by my thigh and sighed wistfully. "I'd love to have my own clinic and not travel so much. To have a house, meet people who could be my friends, but . . ." I shrugged. "With my line of work, it's just not possible. Once people knew where I worked and lived, they'd never leave me alone."

His brow furrowed. "I never considered that."

"Yep, so on the road is how we exist. It's not that bad, though. I've seen most of the country, and I've met people from all walks of life. That would have been impossible if I'd stayed in one spot growing up."

"What about school?"

"I was homeschooled."

"And friends? How did you make friends?"

I plucked a small wildflower from the ground. "I didn't. I don't have many friends, cause like you said, it's hard to meet people when you're always on the go, but I have met a lot of interesting people. That's one perk about traveling."

His eyes twinkled. "Who's the most interesting person you've ever met?"

I pulled another piece of grass and added it to the small bundle in my lap. "If I had to choose just one, I suppose it would be a gypsy woman I met when I was a teenager. She wasn't a client. I met her at a random park we stopped to have lunch in."

Logan's chin tilted my way. "What was interesting about her?"

"Everything. Her clothes, the way she talked, how her body moved. Not only was she beautiful, but there was this ethereal and almost mystical quality to her, like she knew your deepest secrets and at any moment was about to whisper them in your ear." I cocked my head. "The funny thing was, she seemed to *know* about me, about the magic inside me, yet I don't know how she could have since she was a stranger I met at a random rest stop, but she seemed to seek me out. I was sitting on a swing, pouting about something or another as teenagers do, while my mom, nan, and Cecile fixed lunch. That woman approached me, sat on the swing beside me, and said something I've never forgotten."

Logan picked up another pebble and turned it over in

his finger. He cocked an eyebrow, appearing amused. "Are you gonna tell me or leave me hanging?"

I laughed, not able to help it given his expression. "She said that a time would come when I would feel both the dark and the light." I shook my head. "When I asked her what she meant by that, she simply smiled and leaned closer before saying, 'You'll see,' and with that, she stood and walked away. Bells jingled around her ankles as her long black hair swayed around her skirt. Later, when I told my mom about her and asked what she could have meant, my mom didn't have the slightest clue."

"Don't you refer to your magic as light?"

"Yeah, we figured it could be related to my healing light, but we don't have darkness in us, and again, there was no way she could possibly have known about my magic or healing light since she was a random stranger."

Logan frowned, still holding the pebble between his fingers. "Unless she was a psychic," he said quietly.

"A psychic? What do you mean?"

He smiled, his bright white teeth flashing in the sunshine. "Nothing." He pushed up on his elbow more. "So tell me more about you. What kind of stuff do you like? Books? Movies? TV shows? Hobbies?"

I raised my eyebrows, reminding myself that his interest could only be out of politeness and nothing more, but I couldn't stop myself from asking, "Do you usually ask your employers these kinds of things?"

His carefree expression wavered. "No, not usually. Sorry, if you'd rather not tell me—"

"No, it's fine. I'd rather we talk than stare at the grass with awkward silence between us."

Logan chuckled. "Well, when you put it that way."

I laughed.

His gaze stayed twinkling. "So you gonna fill me in on your hobbies?"

I shrugged. "I don't read many books, but I love light fiction—sweet romances or comedies—that kind of stuff. As for movies and TV shows, comedies usually. My line of work can get a little heavy, so keeping my spare time filled with lighter stuff helps."

The wind ruffled the thick dark hair on the top of his head. "That makes sense."

I eyed him shyly. "And you? What do you like?"

"Guy stuff, for the most part. Action movies, spy novels, and crime shows. Although, I can sit through a romantic comedy if I'm asked to."

Probably with Crystal. I pushed that thought away. Logan had no idea that I'd seen his text, so I decided to play dumb. "Does Lila like romantic comedies?"

"On occasion. I'll watch one with her if she asks me to."

"You must be a nice brother. Mike would rather run laps than watch a romantic comedy with Cecile and me, and he doesn't like to run anywhere."

Logan laughed. "Lila does know how to wrap me around her little finger. She can do the same to my dad and brother. It's hard to say no to her, but she's a good kid, if a little spoiled. Since she's the baby in the family, everyone tends to dote on her."

I leaned back on my elbows. "It must be nice to have a sister and a brother. I'd love to have a sibling, but obviously, in my case it's a little different."

Logan's brow knitted. "Why's that?"

I shrugged. "The women in my family only ever have one child. We're a line of women who birth sole daughters. Having a brother or a sister was never in the cards for me."

"Is that part of your magic?"

My lips parted. *Did he just ask about my magic like it was normal? Not even a hint of disbelief?* Being the only supernatural in the world, I was used to skepticism, even derision.

I shook myself. "That's what we think, but honestly, none of us are entirely sure." I patted my belly. "But apparently, the shop closes after we have our daughters."

Logan's gaze strayed to my abdomen then traveled upward to my breasts jutting up toward the sky. He hastily looked away and grabbed another pebble. The small stone was hurtling down the valley before I could blink.

He kept his gaze averted when he said, "So tell me more about you. What's the best place you ever visited?"

I took a deep breath. *Girlfriend, Dar. He has a girlfriend.* "Um . . . maybe the Gulf. We spent time down there one summer . . ."

CHAPTER NINE

The morning drifted by as Logan and I sat in the sunshine talking about everything and anything. As much as I hated to admit it, I was coming to like him. A lot. He was a good listener who seemed genuinely interested in hearing what I had to say, making me wonder if our small talk had turned into genuine interest on his part versus politeness.

Of course, that growing realization only made my predicament worse. It was hard enough dealing with my body's intrinsic attraction to him while knowing he probably had a girlfriend, but also knowing that I genuinely *liked* the guy underneath the sexy packaging was so much harder to deal with.

Another longing filled me as I wished fervently for something that would probably never be.

"You must be hungry," he said after my stomach growled for the second time.

I sheepishly slapped a hand over my abdomen. "I should have had breakfast before we left. My mom always teased me about how loud my stomach can rumble."

He eyed me curiously. "You've never mentioned your father, only your mom." In the sunshine, his dark-brown eyes revealed flecks of gold. "Did he not travel with you?"

I shook my head. "My dad left before I was born. I have no idea who he is."

"I didn't realize."

"It's okay. I don't think about him much anymore. Besides, Mike's been like a dad to me."

"And your mom? Where is she now? To be honest, I've been wondering since you talk about her so much."

My breath caught in my throat as I looked away. "She's, uh, she's dead."

"Oh." His frown deepened. "Sorry. I shouldn't be asking about this kind of stuff—"

"No, it's okay. Really." I forced a brave smile. I grabbed another piece of grass and ran it through my fingers. The small stalk felt coarse and dry.

"Do you . . ." He cleared his throat. "Do you want to talk about it?"

I took a deep breath. *Do I?* I usually never talked about my mom, other than the few random comments I'd made to Logan. Not anymore.

I kept her memory locked away like a closely guarded secret. Part of that was because Cecile and Mike still grieved for her too. Cecile had been my mother's best friend, like the sister she'd never had. And Mike had never admitted it, but I'd always had a hunch he'd been secretly in love with my mother.

Of course, Mike's touch did to my mother what other people's touch did to me. Since he wasn't a mate, she couldn't tolerate it, and he knew that. So, he'd never pushed for anything, but I'd seen him look at her, longingly, lovingly, keeping his feelings and wishes locked inside and only shining through when he thought no one was watching.

I shook my head sadly. One might think talking about her would be how all of us coped, but in reality, usually Cecile and Mike couldn't mention her without getting emotional, and they seemed to think that they needed to be strong for me—not cry or show grief.

Because of that, we'd all fallen into the roles of pretenders. We all pretended that we didn't grieve or cry anymore. Yet the reality of how I felt couldn't be further from that.

Thick emotion wrapped around my throat, like vines choking a plant, and before I thought better of it, I said, "She was my whole world. I loved her so much, and honestly, I feel lost without her." I plucked another wildflower. "My entire world shattered on the day she died."

I could feel Logan watching me, his gaze unwavering. "How did she die?" His quiet, steady words carried on the breeze.

"In a car accident." I swallowed thickly. So far, I'd kept the tears at bay. If I stopped, they would stay there.

I glanced at Logan. He watched me quietly, patiently, letting me decide how much I wanted to reveal.

Seeing that was my undoing. Before I could stop myself, it all came spewing out.

"It was raining that night, a year ago now, when she and my nan died. The accident report said my mom lost control of the car going around an embankment, probably from the wet roads, and they both died at the scene. The paramedics couldn't save either of them. Even if I had been there, I don't know if I could have healed them. One of the paramedics said my nan died on impact and my mom shortly after."

I ripped the grass apart in my lap. "It's a thought that's haunted me ever since. If I had been in the car, if I had survived, would my light have been able to save my family, even if they'd been a second away from death?" I shook my head. "The not knowing drove me mad for so many months. Now, it's just left a gaping hole in my heart. I'll never know."

Logan sat up and inched closer.

I shrugged bitterly. "It's one thing I hate about our gift. We can't heal ourselves. Only other people. My mom couldn't have saved herself."

A moment passed in which I felt his unspoken words, letting me know it was okay to continue, but my emotions had bubbled up so close to the surface, as they always did when I thought about them, that I didn't trust myself to say more. I took a deep, unsteady breath. *Just breathe, Dar.*

Logan shuffled closer, wind whipping through his hair.

His large thighs were only inches away. "I'm really sorry. I can tell that you loved them very much."

"Yeah. I did. I loved them more than anything."

His penetrating gaze felt like embers burning away the outer shell I'd spent the past year erecting around my emotions. Creating that protective bubble had been the only way I'd coped, worked, and survived.

But now, I felt the hard wall encasing my inner grief crumbling in his presence.

Before I could stop it, a tear slipped out. I blinked rapidly as they began to blur my vision. "Sorry! I shouldn't have started. I should have kept my mouth shut. I—"

"It's okay. You can cry." Logan sidled closer, his warm thigh pressing against mine, just as another traitorous tear escaped.

He placed an arm around my shoulders, almost hesitantly, as tears flowed from my eyes in persistent silent rivers.

In the last year, I'd become very good at silent crying. It kept Mike and Cecile from worrying about me if they didn't see how deep my grief went.

In a soft voice, Logan said, "I'm sorry you lost them." His hand drifted down, caressing my back. "I'm really, really sorry."

I tried to reply but couldn't. If I didn't get myself under control, I would be sobbing uncontrollably in seconds.

I closed my eyes and concentrated on the feel of Logan's hand drifting up and down my back. Through my shirt, his hot palm warmed my skin. *Logan's touching me. Actually touching me.*

The dawning realization that Logan's large body was pressing into the side of mine, and all I felt was comfort, created a surreal feeling in my chest. His energy flowed along my skin like a warm cocoon, not penetrating my nerves as my light stayed safely locked away. It was the same reaction as my experiences with him the other day. That only squeezed my heart more.

I wiped my tears on my shirt, dabbing away the moisture on my cheeks. "Have you ever lost anyone?"

"One grandparent, and a few . . . friends but no immediate family like you have."

"You've lost friends?" I peeked up at him through what I assumed were red-rimmed eyes. He either didn't notice my blotchy complexion or was too kind to comment. His sympathetic gaze hadn't lessened.

"Two to be exact, but that was a few years ago." His jaw locked, a haunting shadow coming over his face.

"Were you there?" I asked, assuming they were more military friends.

"Yeah." He dipped his head, his hand still moving up and down my back. It created such a soothing tingle along my skin that I wanted to close my eyes.

"I'm sorry."

He shook his head, the corner of his mouth tilting up sadly. "It was a long time ago, but it's something I'll carry with me until I die, probably similar to you."

"Does it get easier?"

His eyebrows drew together, his gaze drifting to the distant hills. "It gets . . . different. I still think about them, but not every day anymore, but sometimes things happen that remind me of them, then . . ." He shrugged. "Then it comes rushing back but not as intensely as it used to." He paused, his hand still moving steadily along my back. "Someday you'll be able to think of your mom and nan without the intense pain you feel now. It may take a few years, five years, ten years . . . hell, maybe even twenty years, but at some point in the future you'll be able to remember them without it choking you."

My breath rushed out, my gaze dropping to my legs still crisscrossed beneath me. "Do you know this is the first conversation where I've really talked about them since they died?"

"Is that a good thing?"

"Yeah, it is. Just talking about it, telling you about them, in a way, it keeps their memory alive. I think that's what I'm most afraid of. That if I don't speak of them, they'll be forgotten." I swallowed thickly. "And they both deserve to be remembered."

"Are they buried somewhere? Or cremated?"

"They're buried in a cemetery in California. That's where they died."

"Maybe someday I can go there with you."

I snapped my head up.

His expression had once again returned to one filled with calmness and patience. My lips parted. I had no doubt he meant it, that if I truly needed a bodyguard for months, or possibly years, he would one day visit my family's graves with me.

My heart rate picked up. Even though Logan was a potential mate, the memory of Crystal's text flashed to the forefront of my mind.

... miss you. When can you call? I've been ...

I stiffened and inched away, even though I loathed for this moment to end, but guilt bit me hard.

What are you doing, Dar? Making potential plans with Logan? Do you think Crystal would like that her boyfriend is comforting you?

I sat up straighter, desperately trying to bury my emotions for Logan.

His light caresses stopped, his hand pausing mid-movement. Clearing his throat, he pulled his hand away and raked it through his hair, his large bicep as round and hard as a boulder.

I peeked up at him. His dark eyes turned to a stormy sea as he gazed out over the landscape.

I wiped the remaining tears from my cheeks and hastily stood. "We should get back. Mike and Cecile are probably wondering where we are."

Logan nodded, a deep groove appearing between his eyes. "Of course."

He wouldn't meet my gaze when he pushed himself up to stand. The earlier lightheartedness we'd shared had disappeared like dandelion seeds on the breeze.

I swallowed tightly and began walking down the steep hill. Logan's steady footsteps followed.

By the time we reached the bus, a light sheen of sweat covered me, little drops of perspiration pooling between my breasts. But as much as I tried to focus on the physical exertion from the hike, I couldn't stop the images that kept fluttering through my mind—unbidden thoughts of Logan touching me.

Never mind that he had a girl missing him and that we hadn't said two words to one another on the hike down. I kept imagining him with me, *being* with me—being the boyfriend I'd never had.

Images of his large hands sliding over my slick body while his mouth sucked one of my breasts' dusky peaks into his mouth kept entering my thoughts, despite my trying to push them away.

I tried to cut myself some slack. I'd never had such an intensely emotional conversation with any man, and prior to meeting Logan, I'd thought I would be a virgin forever, never able to tolerate a man's touch since I'd never met a potential mate before.

But now . . .

I knew what I was missing. My shoulders sagged. Of all people, I had to react to my bodyguard like that.

But Mom said this is how our magic works. When we find a man who compliments our gift, our bodies know. The light subsides when that happens.

I walked faster as the rest stop building appeared. *And if I can tolerate Logan's touch, surely, there's still hope for me.*

Maybe I could meet another potential mate—a man

who could actually be my boyfriend and didn't have a girl waiting for him at home.

Taking a deep breath, I hopped off the sidewalk to the parking lot. Logan stepped to my side. His forearm brushed mine, almost absentmindedly. From the looks of it, he was deep in thought too.

The open bus door greeted us when we reached it. In the summer months, Mike often left it open to encourage fresh air through our home. Mike and Cecile's conversation from within drifted to my ears. It sounded as if they were having lunch.

My stomach growled again.

I stopped short of the stairs and turned to face Logan.

His head cocked, and he took a step closer to me. "Is everything okay?"

No, everything's not okay. I just told you about my mom, you listened better than anyone I've ever met, and you're a potential mate. I could be with you and be happy. I know it. I can feel it.

I licked my lips, sweat from my upper lip beading on my tongue. Logan's gaze dipped to my mouth before he hastily snapped it away.

"Yeah, everything's fine." I turned and walked inside.

CHAPTER TEN

An hour later, I sat on the couch, a book propped in my lap as I pretended to read. Well, I *tried* to read, but my leg kept jostling, and I had the ridiculous urge to nibble my fingertips.

Since returning from our hike, neither Logan nor I had looked at one another. Instead, we'd climbed aboard the bus, had an awkward lunch with Cecile and Mike, then retreated to opposite ends of the bus. That hadn't lasted long. Within ten minutes of lunch ending, Logan had grabbed his phone and stepped outside.

He'd been talking to someone ever since.

My shoulders slumped. *Probably Crystal.*

The couch cushion dipped when Cecile sat next to me. "Everything okay, Dar?" Her gaze drifted to my forgotten book, then my jostling knee. "Are you fidgeting from the latest email or something else?" She looked out the window at Logan who was pacing the length of the bus with his phone pressed to his ear.

I laughed shrilly, tossing my book aside. "It *should* be from the email, shouldn't it?" Funny how I hadn't given my stalker a second thought since leaving the bus with Logan that morning.

A sympathetic expression covered Cecile's face. She patted my hand before standing. "You never know what the future holds. I know he has a girlfriend, but . . ." She shrugged. "If it's meant to be, it will be."

I smiled, more for her benefit than anything. I knew she was trying to make me feel better, but at the moment, that didn't seem possible.

The bus door hissed, and Logan jumped up the stairs, his mouth tight. Both Cecile and I turned our attention to him.

Logan pocketed his cell phone. "I just got off the phone with those friends of mine. They're going to fly into Billings this afternoon to join us. Alex is certain he can find your stalker, and when we do, I'll need all of them close by."

Cecile's hand drifted to her throat. "You're going to take care of her stalker . . . yourself? Without the police?"

Logan's jaw set. "They're military friends. Don't worry, we have law enforcement ties."

I pulled my bottom lip into my mouth to nibble. *Law enforcement ties? Maybe they're bounty hunters or something.*

Whatever they were, relief that we could avoid the

police with the help of Logan's friends billowed through me, but just as quickly as that relief came, it was replaced by despair.

My lips parted. "But there's no way I can pay all of them. I can barely afford you."

Logan's gaze softened. "You don't need to pay them."

"I don't?"

He shook his head. "As I was telling you, we go way back. When one of us needs something, we're always there for each other. Payment is not something any of them would ask for."

MIKE DROVE us to Billings that afternoon. Since late evening had set in by the time we reached the small city, the sun neared the horizon, and a few stars peeked out. Logan's friends planned to fly into the local airport, so we'd parked in the back of a large strip mall while we waited for them.

I glanced at my watch then tapped my foot. Logan had taken a taxi to the airport and planned to return with all of his friends.

Unlike Cecile and me, Mike seemed more relaxed. Snores drifted toward us as he slumbered in the back, whereas Cecile and I waited anxiously on the couches.

"Here they come." Cecile nodded toward the front windshield.

A small vehicle drove toward us, the outlines of four large men inside.

"Well, they certainly look intimidating." My foot tapped more.

I still wasn't entirely clear on what Logan's friends would do once we found my stalker. His evasive answers every time I asked made my suspicion that they were bounty hunters grow.

But they couldn't know if my stalker was a wanted man, so even if they *were* bounty hunters, it still didn't make sense.

I frowned more. Unless they were mafia, and they simply disposed of creeps?

I gulped. Logan didn't strike me as someone in the mob, but it wasn't as if I had any mafia friends to compare him to.

Car doors slamming filtered through the bus's windows when Logan and his three military buddies emerged from the car. They appeared to be joking around as they slapped each other on their backs or laughed at something one of the others was saying. But that wasn't what caught my attention.

Instead, it was their sheer physical presence. Every single one of them had broad shoulders, muscled arms, large hands, and lean physiques. But their facial characteristics were different.

One was a blond with a ready smile.

Another had brown hair, wore aviator sunglasses, and had a face cut into planes and angles.

And the last had the boy-next-door appeal—brown hair, glasses, and a baseball cap.

But despite their being Logan's friends whom he trusted with his life, they were still strangers to me.

And I was about to live with them.

Logan's gaze caught mine through the windshield. My breath stopped. The way his chocolate-brown irises bored into me, as if he could sense all of the turmoil and uncertainty coursing through my veins, made me want to squirm and wring my hands even more.

Logan's expression turned serious, and he said something to his friends. All three of them glanced my way.

That just made my cheeks flush more.

"Should we greet our guests?" Cecile smoothed her slacks.

"Um, yeah."

Knowing our accommodation was about to grow more crowded with the addition of those three, I hurried forward, intending to rush outside so I could properly introduce myself in the wide open.

I slammed my hand against the door's release button, but in my hurry to get outside, I tripped on the stairs. My eyes widened with horror as my limbs flailed. Before I knew what was happening, I was sailing down the stairs headfirst.

A shriek escaped me just before a strong pair of arms encircled my torso. Those arms flipped me upright and cradled me against a broad chest.

My breath caught in my throat. Tingles of light shot through me, like meteors blazing across the sky.

"Whoa, there." The deep voice held a hint of amusement. "Logan told us you were eager to catch a stalker, but I didn't realize how eager."

With burning cheeks, I tilted my face up.

Cool blue eyes met mine. A smile came next. All I registered was a handsome face, straight teeth, and blond hair.

I struggled, trying to dislodge myself from his arms. My light had burst out of the storage chest in my belly, and painful electric sparks shot along my limbs.

Logan cleared his throat and said in a gruff voice, "Brodie, are you going to set her down?"

Brodie finally set me on my feet. The feel of his hard chest disappeared. Beneath my soles, the world finally stopped spinning.

Brodie grinned again, his face only inches from mine. "You must be Daria?" He gave a low whistle. "Wow! Logan didn't tell us what a knockout you are. Do you know you have the most beautiful eyes I've ever seen?"

I brought a hand to my forehead. The aftereffects of that much direct touch still lingered. "Ah, thanks."

Brodie grinned. "And I have to say, that was quite the introduction."

My cheeks heated.

"I can't say I mind. It's not every day an attractive woman lands in my arms."

Logan glowered at Brodie before abruptly stepping in front of me, blocking Brodie from view. "Daria, these are the friends I was telling you about. You've already met Brodie."

Brodie chuckled, sidestepping Logan so I could see him again. He seemed to find Logan's annoyed tone amusing. "Nice to meet ya, Daria."

Logan grumbled under his breath before gesturing to the other two men. "And these two are Jake and Alexander."

The ones standing by Logan's side nodded politely and murmured, "Ma'am." They stood with duffel bags slung over their shoulders.

Jake was wearing aviator sunglasses, while Alexander had a baseball cap shielding his eyes.

They seemed more reserved than Brodie, who was still grinning, and they didn't really seem like mafia nor did I feel threatened by them. If anything, a warm feeling of being completely safe with them slid through me.

"It's nice to meet you too. Thanks for coming."

"Not a problem." Jake took off his sunglasses. Piercing, deep-set hazel eyes met mine. He was more angular than Logan and had cheekbones any supermodel would die for.

"We hear some guy's giving you trouble?" Alexander pulled my attention to him. A baseball cap hid most of his brown hair, and glasses perched on his nose. He had such a boy-next-door wholesomeness to him that the lingering embarrassment over my fall ebbed away.

"That's right. It started a few weeks ago."

Logan nodded at Alexander. "Alex is the one who's

good with computers. With his help, we should be able to track down your stalker."

Footsteps tapped from within the bus, and Cecile and Mike appeared at the top of the stairs. I knew Cecile had witnessed my fall because of her muffled scream, but I never would have guessed it now. She appeared entirely composed and serene—so very *Cecile*.

Cecile descended; her willowy form as elegant and composed as a duchess being announced at a ball. She extended her hand to shake first Brodie's hand then the others', her gaze warm, her words welcoming.

Mike yawned before doing the same, but his yawning stopped when he looked Logan and his friends up and down. Each of them towered over six feet and had shoulders wide enough to brush a doorway.

"Well, nice to meet you fellas." He hefted his jeans over his belly before patting his paunch. "You boys make me think I should hit the gym more."

Jake smiled crookedly. "Working out is part of our job."

I cocked my head. *They have to work out for their job? Does that mean they work security like Logan?*

Mike chuckled. "Well, driving's my job. Not exactly great for the six-pack."

Brodie laughed.

As the seven of us stood in the parking lot, cars occasionally driving by and the sun sinking below the horizon, it struck me for the first time that I was about to embark on something I'd never experienced before—hanging out with new people in an enclosed spaced. That was something I usually avoided since it wreaked havoc on my gift, but it would be necessary while we tried to track down the man who wanted me dead.

But Lord help me, I'd never lived so closely with so many drop-dead gorgeous men.

CHAPTER ELEVEN

"These are the kinds of emails this prick's been sending you?" Alexander asked from the couch.

Brodie and Jake sat beside him, peering over his shoulder at my laptop. They reminded me of sardines packed tightly into a can.

Alexander had taken his hat off, revealing startling blue eyes behind his glasses and a heavy brow. Muscled forearms rested on his thighs while the computer lay in his lap. His gaze traveled over the emails as he scanned them one by one, his earlier boyish cuteness gone as his jaw became a hard edge.

"That's right. Thirteen so far," Logan replied. He sat beside me on the opposite couch. My senses were acutely aware of him.

Cecile and Mike stood near the kitchen, watching on anxiously.

"What a crazy mofo." Brodie shook his head, his mouth tight.

"No kidding." Jake's hazel eyes flashed darkly.

"Scary stuff," Alexander added. "Seems like a real psycho."

My stomach tightened. "Exactly, which is why I want to figure out who he is. Is that possible?"

Alexander nodded and leaned forward. "I'll find him."

I eyed him curiously. "Can I ask how?"

He angled the laptop screen in my direction, my email already pulled up. "Through his messages. Most emails have information in what's called an 'email header' that's normally hidden. But if you know a thing or two about computers, you can find out all sorts of information about someone."

Alexander pulled up an email from Cecile and showed me what lay within an email header. My eyes widened when I took in page after page of technical gibberish.

"You can understand that?"

"Lucky for you, yeah." He pointed at the screen. "See here? This tells me that Cecile emailed you from her smartphone, a Samsung device. And here? This tells me what router it went through. Using that info, I just pull up this handy-dandy site." He pasted the IP address into a browser. "This site gives me the longitude and latitude of where Cecile was when she sent that email, so I have a fairly good idea where she was when she sent it."

I grinned. "That's amazing! So you can definitely find where my stalker lives!"

"Should be able to." Alexander pulled up my stalker's emails. His fingers flew across the keyboard, and technical gibberish appeared. He paused, scratching his chin. "Or not. The creep emailing you seems to know a thing or two about tech, cause he's using a VPN."

My grin vanished. "What's a VPN?"

"A virtual private network. VPNs route internet traffic through their own servers, so instead of seeing his actual IP address, I'll see something else instead that points me to Russia or France or some other country. Obviously, that's not where he actually is."

"Oh." My shoulders fell. "Then how do we find him?"

Alexander rolled up his sleeves, a devilish smile growing on his face. "This is where it gets fun. Since he's not playing nice, I'm not going to, either."

Brodie chuckled. "Don't get him started. The dude seriously gets off on this stuff."

Jake's lips twitched up. "Daria, I think it's safe to say you're in good hands. Sooner or later, Alexander will find him."

"But how?" I persisted.

"I'm going to drop a few phishing emails to start off with. All I need him to do is click the link. Once he does, I'm in and can access everything on his hard drive. Even if he's careful about what he stores, most likely, I'll still be able to find something on him that will allude to his identity."

I breathed a sigh of relief that Alexander obviously

knew what he was doing. "Thank you. Honestly, I can't thank you enough."

He pushed his glasses up, the cute-boy-next-door appeal back. "Not a problem. This is kinda what I do."

Logan inched closer. "Just let us handle it, Dar. We've all dealt with creeps like this before. We know how to get to the bottom of it."

I smiled at him even though I wondered *how* they would deal with my stalker once they found him, but gratitude still flooded me. "Thank you." I reached over and squeezed Logan's hand. As soon as I did it, I couldn't believe what I'd done.

Logan stared down at our hands, his entire body going still.

You did not just do that! I hastily snatched my hand away, heat rushing up my neck. *Is this another potential mate thing? That I randomly touch men who are actually off limits?*

Logan's gaze stayed on his thigh, where our joined hands had been. The rigidness in his posture didn't ease.

Brodie cleared his throat.

My cheeks heated even more when it became apparent that everyone was staring at us. Cecile and Mike's jaws had dropped.

Nervously, I threaded my hand through my long, blond hair. A few wavy strands fell across my shoulder. Logan continued to sit there, unmoving.

Brodie leaned back against the couch, a curious glint in his eye before he slung an arm over the couch back.

THE MOON BATHED the sky in silvery light. Snores filled the bus as I lay in my bed. It seemed not only Mike snored, but Jake did too.

At the front of the bus, bright light from Alexander's laptop illuminated his and Logan's faces as they tried to find more information on my stalker.

They probably thought they were the only ones awake, but I couldn't sleep. Too much had happened. Not only had Logan called in his friends to help, but I'd also accepted what had been staring me in the face ever since I'd met my bodyguard.

Logan Smith was a potential mate, the first potential mate I'd ever met, and I had an insanely stupid, completely ridiculous, mind-blowing crush on him. I groaned in despair. I was crushing for him so hard that one would think I was a thirteen-year-old girl who'd just entered puberty.

Up the aisle, Logan's broad shoulders were visible from where he sat on the couch. He looked like a wall of concrete—hard and immobile.

I itched to touch him, to run my fingers along the hard planes of his back, to feel his muscles jump and dance beneath my fingertips.

But despite my interest in him, interest that Brodie had obviously picked up on, given his knowing smirks during the evening, Logan hadn't said a word about it.

Duh. He's got a girlfriend, he's obviously loyal, and he's still doing his job while tolerating your blubbering actions.

I pushed deeper under my covers as tapping from Alexander's keyboard drifted my way.

I needed to stop thinking about Logan. As soon as my stalker was caught, Logan would be on his way, returning to his normal life, a life that didn't include me. But I still couldn't stop my feelings.

It was completely insane that only three days had passed since I'd met him, because one thing was growing increasingly apparent to me—I was falling for Logan hard and fast—and it would only end in tears.

WHEN MORNING FINALLY ARRIVED, my eyes felt heavy and lethargic, but the scent of coffee made me stir. However, it was Brodie's abrupt "He emailed again!" that had me bolting upright in bed.

A quick assessment of my surroundings showed no one else in their bunks. The floor was also empty. I distinctly remembered Jake occupying that space, but his rolled-up sleeping bag and pillow lay neatly folded by the bathroom.

The top bunk squeaked in protest as I scrambled to get out from under the sheets. "He did? What did he say?" I fumbled with the covers and pushed them off.

It was only when I nearly collided with Brodie, Logan, and the other two at the front of the bus that I realized each of the guys—except Mike—was staring at my chest. When I glanced down, my jaw dropped in horror.

My damned nipples were once again erect and poking through the thin fabric of my pajama top.

Since I was wearing shorts that had a whopping inseam of two inches, I wasn't exactly covered in that department either.

I hastily crossed my arms as embarrassment stained my cheeks red.

Logan's gaze whipped to his friends, and his eyebrows drew together in a dark scowl. He stepped in front of me, his body shielding me from them. Broad shoulders cut off my view.

"What were you saying, Brodie?" Logan placed his hands on his hips.

Brodie, Alexander, and Jake all cleared their throats. I peeked under Logan's bent arm. His friends all hastily shifted their gazes to anywhere but me.

"Um . . . I . . ." Brodie's stammered reply only made Logan's scowl deepen.

A hooded sweatshirt draped across one of the couches. Without considering whose it was, I grabbed it and threw it on. A whiff of sandalwood floated up to greet me. That scent solidified its owner. Glancing Logan's way, I cocked my head to see if he minded.

He caught my subtle communication and nodded.

"So what does it say?" I zippered the sweatshirt all the way to my throat and crossed my arms. The ginormous garment fell to mid-thigh, effectively swallowing me in a thick cottony curtain.

"I don't know. I haven't opened it yet," Alexander replied.

I perched on the couch's arm. Logan's scowl lessened when he sat down by Alexander, his shoulder brushing my thigh. Jake and Brodie continued to keep their attention diverted from me.

Wow. Logan's sway over his friends was rather impressive.

Shoving off that realization, I propped my hand on the couch back and leaned into my palm, over Logan and Alexander. Brodie and Jake stayed on Alexander's other side, their gazes glued to the laptop.

"Here goes nothing." Alexander clicked the email, and it popped open.

My breath sucked in when I saw the familiar greeting.

Dear Ms. Gresham,

Tick tock. Tick tock, witch. Since you haven't paid, the day is coming . . .

By the way, I left a present for you. It's just outside. A little hint of what's to come if you ultimately don't pay.

Your biggest fan.

My breath stopped, my heart rate picking up. "A present?"

I shot to standing, but Logan was already up and

striding toward the front door, Alexander, Jake, and Brodie hot on his heels.

Mike and Cecile watched from near the kitchen, bewildered expressions on their faces.

I stumbled after the guys, my heart jackhammering against my ribs. *Oh God. Oh God. Oh God.* Panic welled up in my chest, threatening to suffocate me.

The bus door hissed open. Logan and his friends were out the door before I could blink. A part of me wanted to run, to escape to the back of the bus and pretend that nothing waited for me outside, but the other part had to see.

Morbid curiosity pushed me forward, despite Cecile's protests and the low hum of conversation already taking place between Logan and his friends.

"Dar, maybe you should wait here!" Cecile tried to reach for me, but I brushed her off.

I moved on stiff legs, sweat already breaking out across my forehead.

"Is that real or . . ." Brodie's sentence cut off.

The blood whooshing through my ears made hearing difficult, but I caught Jake's reply.

"Yes, but the *real* question is, how did he find us?"

Somehow, I managed to not pass out. Below me, Logan gripped what looked like a small box.

His friends crowded around him.

"What's in there?" My voice came out in a high squeak.

Logan swung around, his jaw locked and his nostrils flaring. Once again, I caught a hint of the man he was. A shiver ran through me. If I'd bumped into him on the street while he wore that expression, I would have run the other way.

"Nothing. Stay inside."

His clipped tone made me want to retreat, but once again, my legs didn't listen. I took the steps down slowly, as if I were floating down an escalator.

Logan shoved the box into Jake's hand and turned, blocking me from exiting the bus. "I mean it, Dar. Stay inside."

"No." The quiet word left my lips like a battle line drawn. "I want to see what he sent me."

Logan stepped closer, his face softening, but that angry storm still brewed just beneath the surface, even though he was trying to hide it. He gently placed a hand on my waist, trying to propel me back inside and up the stairs.

If I hadn't been so scared, I would have shivered when his large palm grazed my skin, but all I could do was stare at the closed box in Jake's hand.

"Dar. Please," Logan said hoarsely.

But I stepped past him and stopped in front of Jake who glanced over my shoulder, presumably at Logan, as if asking for permission or guidance on what to do. Before Logan could tell him, I snatched the box from Jake's hand and flung it open.

My eyes grew wide. I shrieked and dropped the box as my hands came to my mouth. I stumbled backward, right into Logan's hard chest as his arms enclosed around me.

"Is that real? Is it really *real?*" Even to my ears, I sounded on the verge of hysteria.

Logan swung me around and scooped me into his arms. Before I knew what was happening, the air whooshed past me, and I was sailing up the stairs and into the bus, past Mike and Cecile on the way to the back.

But none of that registered. All I could see was the blood.

Blood.

Feathers.

The scent of rotting flesh.

Oh god. Oh god. Oh god. He's going to kill me. He's really going to kill me!

My breath came so fast. Too fast.

"Breathe, Dar. Just breathe." Logan sat beside me on the bottom bunk. The feel of the mattress dipping beneath us registered faintly in my mind. The only other thing I felt was Logan's large hand on my back, rubbing up and down as he tried to soothe me. "It's going to be fine."

His deep, calm words helped clear my head. Just the feel of him beside me, his hard thigh pressing into mine, elicited a wave of relief. I scooted closer to him, craving the feel of him—needing it.

"He killed that bird and beheaded it? Didn't he?"

Logan's jaw worked. "Apparently, yeah, he did."

"But how did he find me? How did he find me, Logan? How could he have possibly known where I was?" That suffocating feeling worked up my throat again.

His jaw worked more. "I don't know."

I reached for his hand and grasped it before I thought better of it. His fingers entwined with mine. They were hard and calloused.

I closed my eyes and leaned closer to him, breathing in his scent.

My heartbeat slowed.

"That poor bird," I finally murmured when I felt grounded enough to speak.

Inside the box had lain a large beheaded pigeon. Blood had congealed around its neck, and one leg had appeared broken. I had no idea if my stalker had broken the leg before or after he'd killed the bird.

I wasn't sure I wanted to know.

I took another deep breath, concentrating on the feel of Logan's hand. "He's really going to kill me, isn't he? If I don't pay him, he'll come after me, and he knows how to find me."

Logan's jaw locked, and the hard, sinewy muscles in his thighs clenched. "No. He won't get anywhere near you. We'll catch him."

"But what if you don't?"

"We will."

"Logan?" Alexander called from the front of the bus. "We have a few ideas but wanted to run them by you. Can you come up here?"

Logan swung toward me, his expression stormy. "Stay here. Inside the bus. Okay? We'll take care of this."

I let go of his hand, missing the feel of him immediately. I nodded shakily. "Yeah. Okay, I'll stay back here."

He nodded curtly, then stood and stalked to the front before flying down the stairs to join his friends outside.

Cecile and Mike finally kicked into action from where they'd been frozen by the kitchen. They hurried to my side, Cecile making crooning noises while Mike readjusted his Yankees cap again and again.

"It's all right, Dar. It's okay. This is why we hired Logan. He'll take care of it." She said the words over and over, as if trying to reassure me and herself.

Mike still looked bewildered. "But how did he know we were here? How could he know that?" He twisted his hat more.

Cecile shot him a sharp look. "Right now, that's not important. What's important is staying calm and preparing for Daria's next show."

My show. Right. I'd completely forgotten about that.

Thumping sounded from the front of the bus when Logan and Alexander climbed the steps. Jake and Brodie were nowhere to be seen.

I shot to standing. "Well? What's the plan?"

Logan joined me, that formidable expression once again in place, making me shiver. "Brodie and Jake have left to check into a few things. They'll meet us later, before your show starts."

"What are they going to check into?"

"They're going to try to track down how that package arrived here. You know, looking into any surveillance around here and asking those who also stayed the night if they saw anything. They'll catch up with us later."

I wrapped my arms around myself and sat back down, some of my tension leaving. I wasn't alone. I needed to remember that. Logan and his friends knew what they were doing. They would keep us safe.

Alexander crouched down at my side. "The good news is that he emailed again, so we still have an open line of communication."

"Have you been able to track down where he lives?"

"Not yet. He hasn't picked up the bait, but that doesn't mean that he won't."

"So what's the plan now?" Cecile asked. She clasped her shaky hands. "Daria's clients arrive in four hours. We'll need to set up at our next venue."

Logan sat at my side again, the mattress sinking toward him. "We'll carry on as planned, but until Jake and Brodie return, I don't want her seeing anyone. I'd feel better if all four of us were guarding her."

I drew my knees up inside Logan's sweatshirt and looped my arms around them.

"I'll . . . uh . . . get the bus started so we can head out." Mike frowned heavily but looked relieved to have a job to do. When he reached the front and turned the ignition, a loud rumble vibrated the bunk.

"All right then." Cecile smoothed her hair with a shaky hand, tucking a few wayward strands behind her ears. "We should be at the magic shop within twenty minutes since we're so close. Do you need time to prepare, Daria?"

I fidgeted then stood. My mood still felt on the verge of panic as another show loomed. But stalker or not, people were counting on me. I couldn't let them down. "No. I'm fine. I'll just freshen up and get dressed."

Logan stood, his large hands steadying me when I began shaking again. The feel of his large palms encircling my biceps made heat that had nothing to do with the warm clothing race up my limbs.

I had the ridiculous urge to lean into him again. Straightening, I gave him what I hoped was a brave smile. "I'm good. Really. I am."

"Do you feel up to this?"

I swallowed uneasily. "Yeah. I'll be absolutely fine." The lie slipped out easily.

Logan turned to Cecile, his hands dropping from around me. "How many clients does she have on the schedule today?"

She already had her clipboard out. Despite my trying to coax her into the twenty-first century, she still preferred pen and paper. "Only fifteen today, so a normal day."

"And Lucy?" I asked, standing up straighter, grateful for the distraction. Another image of that dead bird flitted through my mind, and I grimaced, trying to dispel the image. "Is she on the schedule today?"

Cecile hovered her pen over the paper. "She's number one."

I nodded tightly. Then that meant I had no choice but to work.

I couldn't let her down again.

CHAPTER TWELVE

All seven of us stood in the back storage room of the magic shop. The cramped space held layers of dust, and dust motes flew in the air. A single light illuminated the room, casting shadows into the corners. Shelves lined with boxes took up most of the space.

While it was crowded, it also felt secure: only two exit doors and no windows. Logan seemed happy about that.

Jake and Brodie had returned a few hours after we'd arrived in our latest small town, their expressions grim. Apparently, my stalker had covered his tracks. No one had seen him, and the rest stop didn't have security cameras.

Logan had scowled, cursing quietly when they divulged that information, but the magic shop's owner, a man named Peter, was none the wiser about my terrifying morning. He grinned as he showed us around.

"It's truly a pleasure to have you here!" Peter wore thick

glasses that rested on his bulbous red nose. He hadn't stopped grinning since we'd arrived, following me around like an eager puppy as I surveyed our workspace. "My wife couldn't believe it when I told her I booked a real magician."

I stifled a sneeze and gave him a smile. "I'm not sure I'd call myself a magician." I swallowed a cough from the dust, and even though I was trying my best to act normal around Peter, my nerves still felt fried from the morning.

"But what else *would* you call it?" Peter laughed. "You're the real deal, not like most I see." He hunkered closer and said in a conspiring tone, "We have a few in the area who fancy themselves professionals, but I can assure you they're not." He laughed, his large belly moving up and down with each inhalation.

I bit back a genuine smile despite a steady thrum of nervousness going through me. We only had thirty minutes before Lucy was due to arrive, and nothing was set up.

As if sensing my distress, Brodie clapped Peter on the shoulder. "She's a *supernatural healer extraordinaire*, a very coveted title, one that takes years of study to earn." He steered the owner away, going on about some made-up magic school I'd attended.

Peter soaked up every word, his grin broadening with each step they took. Brodie shut the door to the front of the shop firmly behind him, dimming the morning sunshine that streamed in through the shop's front windows.

Logan stepped to my side, his dark eyes fixed on my mouth. I'd pulled my lip between my teeth to nibble. My tongue darted out to lick my lips as I became acutely aware of how close he stood.

He abruptly straightened and shifted his gaze. "Why don't you let us set up? Take some time to get ready. We'll have this place good to go in no time. Just stay in here so I know where you are."

Before I could protest that I could help, too, Logan addressed Alexander and Jake. "Boys? Let's get a move on."

All of them seemed tenser, as if realizing that my stalker really *did* pose a threat. He wasn't just some weirdo hiding behind threatening emails.

The three of them disappeared out the back door, their shoulders brushing the doorway. The closing door caused a rush of cool morning air to flow into the cramped storage room.

We'd parked the bus in the lot behind the shop and planned to spend the night there. Peter had been more than happy to clear the parking spots for us.

As I rested, mentally preparing for the day to come, Logan and his friends carried three, sometimes four, boxes in at a time. The bed, chairs, small tables, candles, sheets, snacks, drinks, and other items we offered to keep clients comfortable appeared. They had everything set up in ten minutes, a feat that would have taken Cecile, Mike, and me an hour.

Jake dusted his hands off. "All done then?" His nose

wrinkled when he stepped closer to a shelf. It held jars of fake pickled troll heads.

Cecile stepped back into the room from the outside, clipboard in hand. "We're ready to go. Daria's first client arrives in fifteen minutes. It will be another busy day for her." Her hand shook as she held her pencil. Try as she might to hide her emotions, anxiety over the latest threat seemed to be affecting her as well.

Logan crossed his arms. His biceps were so big, they reminded me of grapefruits. "The four of us will cover all entries and exits to this building. Alexander also brought a metal detector. We'll be using that on everyone after we pat them down."

Cecile brought a hand to her throat. "A metal detector?" She gave a nervous laugh.

I tried to calm the anxiety in my voice, but it came through anyway. "Well, that's a first."

Logan growled softly and stepped closer. "We'll keep you safe. Don't worry about security. Let me deal with that."

Lucy and her husband arrived right on time. Similar to the other day, she draped from her husband's arm like a sickly accessory. She coughed weakly when she entered the dusty room, the back door closing behind her. Alexander stood watch in the back parking lot.

The scented candles flickered in the draft when the door closed.

"Let me help you." I rushed forward to support her negligible weight until she was safely lying on the portable bed.

Logan stood nearby, his gaze following my every move. He stayed quiet, but his presence was palpable. Lucy's husband kept glancing nervously over his shoulder at Logan.

Lucy gripped my hand tightly once she was supine. "I'm so happy you could see me today. Please help me."

Tingles shot through my arm at her touch, but I ignored it. With my free hand, I smoothed back her short, wispy hair. "I will."

Lucy's face flushed as she glanced upward. "Chemo did that," she said, waving her free hand at her hair, "but even the chemo couldn't stop my cancer."

"I don't need drugs to help people." I smiled, trying to put her at ease. "Now, should we begin?"

"Please. It hurts everywhere."

A door opened, and out of the corner of my eye, I saw Brodie enter. A flash of sunlight came with him before he closed the door firmly behind him and backed up to it, arms crossed.

His immense bulk would stop anyone from entering from that direction, and with Alexander outside guarding the back parking lot, and Logan standing close by while Jake prowled the shop's perimeter, no one would be bothering us.

My shoulders relaxed.

"Let's begin." I held my hands over her. "Lucy, I'd like you to close your eyes. You may feel a hot, burning sensation, but it won't hurt you. It will heal you."

Lucy's eyelids fluttered closed. Her thin, birdlike arms lay listlessly at her sides. Sharp bones protruded from her wrists, and her wedding ring hung limply from an emaciated finger. Only the larger knuckle kept it in place.

I shifted my hands above her. Sick black energy swirled into my palms. *So many tumors.* My heart broke for her. The cancer had metastasized deep within her bones. It was everywhere. *No wonder she's in so much pain.*

Closing my eyes, I moved my palms over her length—shifting and swaying until my light told me exactly where every cancer cell lay. "I'm going to start now."

I called upon the firelight within me until flames consumed my insides. Pain shot down my arms and into my fingertips. Biting my lip, I resisted the urge to yelp.

Sweat grew on my brow as I gritted my teeth tightly. *The cancer goes so deep!*

Minutes passed as I extracted the disease from Lucy's sick body. The illness flowed relentlessly into me, making my arms shake.

Lucy's body grew lighter as I scaled out the tumors. The ugly cancerous masses that had been eating her insides flowed into me, and the rotting, gelatinous disease swam through my veins, like jelly that wanted to clog my pores and eat my insides.

When I was certain I had extracted every cancer cell in

her body, I dropped my hands. My chest rose and fell as I took ragged breaths. Excruciating pain consumed me.

You knew this one wouldn't be easy.

Rot filled my organs, my blood, and every cell of my being. The cancer was everywhere.

I called up my healing light again, coaxing and growing the fire. More sweat trickled down my face in a hot salty river. *So many tumors!*

It took every ounce of my concentration to rid myself of them, but as soon as I thought I had them all, my light would alert me to another cell, another mass. I gritted my teeth. *Keep going.*

A part of me was vaguely aware of Lucy calling my name, but I couldn't reply.

There's too many! I fell to the ground, the strain becoming too much.

"What the hell?" someone called in a deep voice. Hands wrapped around me.

I cried out.

"What's going on?" Logan's snarl filled the room. "Why hasn't that light come from her fingertips?"

A small part of me was aware of Logan supporting my body, but I was still fighting so hard to rid myself of the cancer that the thought was there then gone, like a passing car in the night.

"Sometimes the disease is too great," Cecile replied quietly. "Then Daria needs extra time."

I opened my eyes to see Cecile hunkering down in front of me as a sickly feeling swept through my body. *There are still tumors inside me!* Logan's hands steadied my upper body. They felt hot and oddly comforting. I leaned more into him. Nausea rolled through me.

He supported my weight easily. "Daria?" he asked anxiously. "What can I do?"

I still panted. The amount of energy it had taken to rid Lucy of her disease was vastly more than I'd anticipated. Swallowing down the nausea, I replied, "Can you help me to my feet?"

Logan stood, with me gently supported in his arms until I was standing again. His hard body pressed into me from behind as his hands steadied my upper arms. From the feel of it, he had no intention of letting go.

Lucy was sitting upright on the table. Gone were the pale skin and lackluster expression. A look of hope and wonder filled her face. Her husband stood just behind her, tears shimmering in his eyes.

"I feel . . ." Lucy's eyes misted over. "Healthy and pain free and . . ." She turned around to grip her husband's hands. "I'm cured. I know it! I know she cured me! I don't feel sick anymore!"

She threw her arms around him, her movements fast and strong. He gripped her tightly in return.

Over Lucy's shoulder, his gaze met mine. I stood quietly, weak and still sick, against Logan.

"I don't . . ." Lucy's husband shook his head and cleared his throat. "I don't know how we can ever thank you. You've . . ." His voice trembled, and he sniffed. "You've given me my wife back."

Lucy let go of her husband to face me. Happiness beamed in her grin. "Thank you! Thank you so much!" She flung her arms around me before I could stop her.

I groaned quietly at the assault. Her arms gripped me too tightly, pressing my bones and making the pain that resided there flare.

"Oh! I'm sorry! I didn't mean to—"

Cecile pried Lucy away from me. "That's quite all right, but Daria needs some time to herself right now. She still needs to work her magic."

Lucy's face fell. "Is she okay?"

Cecile's strained smile stretched. "She will be, but right now, she's not."

Before Lucy could reply, Cecile ushered Lucy and her husband to the door. Brodie already had it open, his brow furrowed as he watched me.

Once they left the room, I collapsed against Logan again.

"Daria? What's going on?" Fear filled my bodyguard's voice.

"I still have her cancer inside me."

His body turned as hard as a rock. "Her cancer is inside *you?*"

I winced at his sharp tone. "Yes. That's how I heal people. I take their sickness into me and rid them of it."

"Holy shit," Brodie murmured quietly.

"So you're sick now?" Logan lifted me until I sat on my healing table, anxiety in his eyes. "Until your light what? Eats it away?"

I smiled wanly. "Something like that."

A sharp knock came at the door Brodie guarded. He lifted his head and sniffed. "It's Cecile."

I cocked my head in surprise. *Did he just smell Cecile?* Before I could ponder that, the door burst open and Cecile rushed back inside. She pushed Logan out of the way until she stood directly in front of me.

"Daria? Sweetheart, you need to concentrate." Her hands fluttered over my face, pushing back the sweaty tendrils of hair.

I closed my eyes. Fatigue rolled through me. "I know. How long until my next client?"

Her nervous movements didn't stop. "Don't worry about that. You just rid yourself of the disease first."

Despite Cecile taking over, Logan hadn't gone far. He lingered just off to the right, looking every bit as fearful and worried as he had two seconds ago.

"What the hell's going on?" he asked. "Does she really have cancer?"

Cecile gave a slight nod. "In a way, yes. Daria now has Lucy's sickness inside her."

The energy off Logan increased tenfold. He raked a hand angrily through his hair again and began to pace.

"Logan!" Cecile said sharply. "Daria needs to concentrate right now. If she doesn't, the sickness will spread until she's too weak to consume it."

That statement stopped Logan in his tracks. He gulped, his Adam's apple bobbing. "What do you need me to do?" he asked in a hoarse whisper.

"Stand back and stay calm." Cecile's cool hands settled against my cheeks as she felt my skin. "Lie back, Daria." She guided me down on the table. "Close your eyes and take a few deep breaths. You know what you need to do."

I did as she said, but it was hard. Cecile was right. Already, the sickness was growing inside me, the cancer trying to dominate my light.

Closing my eyes, I turned inward in deep concentration. Through the fog that swirled in my brain, quiet words registered.

"What happens if she can't consume it?" Logan asked softly.

A moment passed before Cecile said in a shaky voice, "Then she dies."

CHAPTER THIRTEEN

Trembles shook my body like vibrations from a shock wave. It wasn't the first time something like this had happened, but I didn't remember it ever being so hard to rid myself of an illness. Lucy had been sicker than I imagined. She would likely have died within days if I hadn't cured her.

Concentrate, Daria. Don't let the cancer beat you. I called upon the firelight inside me. It glowed brightly, as hot as the sun. My brow furrowed as sweat erupted on my forehead. *Kill the cells, Daria. Kill them all.*

The world around me took on another dimension. Everything disappeared as if falling into a cosmic void. Fatigue rolled through my body as the light, once again, relentlessly tracked down every cancer cell. They were trying to hide. The sickness wanted to burrow deep within my bones and organs. The lapse of my light, when I hadn't been able to concentrate, had made the surviving tumors stronger.

Minutes or hours passed. I couldn't tell which. It took every ounce of power within me to fight and consume the disease. It seemed to take forever until the last cell finally vanished.

When the last of the disease faded, my light glowed hotter and brighter—as if triumphant at my win—before it burst from my fingertips. I sagged in relief.

"Thank God," Logan whispered hoarsely.

Sometime in the past minute, I'd become aware of him again. Despite my eyes being closed, I felt him crouching at my side, completely silent but very much *there*. His worry and fear filled the room.

I opened my eyes.

"Daria?" His eyebrows drew sharply together. "Are you okay?"

Cecile, Mike, and Brodie hovered to the side.

"Yes. I'm good." My voice was quiet but firm. "That was a hard one."

Logan sighed heavily. "I thought . . ."

His head dropped, his breathing still ragged, before he abruptly straightened and reached behind my back to help me sit up, his large hand splayed between my shoulder blades.

Even in my weakened state, I responded to him. Shivers ran down my spine.

"So you're okay now?" His brown eyes skimmed over

my features, as if assessing me for some illness that could sprout up at any moment.

I bit back a tired smile. His worry reminded me of a fretting hen. "Yes, I'm fine. Really, I am." Taking a deep breath, I turned to Cecile. "When is my next client due?"

"No!" Logan's growl made Cecile jump. "There's no way you're seeing anyone else today!"

"I'll be fine, Logan. This is what I do for a living."

He guffawed. "You almost *die* for a living?"

"What just happened is abnormal. That's not how it usually goes."

"But you could have—"

"It's okay." More than anything, I wanted to lean into him and press my lips against his.

He growled, and that strange light glowed in his eyes.

My lips parted. *What causes that light?*

"I think you should rest. Your clients can wait a few hours."

Before I could respond, Logan scooped me into his arms and began issuing orders to Brodie who didn't even blink, as if Logan's over-protective nature were normal.

It wasn't until we'd exited the back of the magic shop and the summer breeze rolled across my cheeks that my mouth began working.

"Logan! Put me down!"

His long strides ate up the sidewalk.

I struggled, but his grip only tightened. Exasperated, I crossed my arms awkwardly. "Logan, you need to put me down so I can work!"

"I *will* put you down, just as soon as we're on the bus."

The bus door hissed open, and he sprinted up the stairs, taking them in two giant leaps. I was breathless by the time he deposited me on the couch.

"You can't—" I pushed my hair back from my face. "I mean, I know you're worried, but you can't force me to stop."

"I can, and I will. My job is to protect you, even if that means protecting you from yourself."

Alexander and Jake had joined Brodie by the bus's door. The three of them stood with their arms crossed, as if guarding our home. Cecile and Mike stood in front of them. Neither of them looked very worried, but Cecile did check her watch a few times.

My next client must be due soon. I couldn't let them down.

I stood from the couch, intent on marching back down the stairs, but I swayed. Bringing a hand to my forehead, I used my other hand to steady myself against the wall.

Logan stepped closer to me. "See? You shouldn't be working. You're in no shape to heal anyone right now."

I gritted my teeth in frustration and sat down in a huff on the couch. "But I do this all the time."

He kneeled in front of me. In a softer tone, he said, "But even you said this morning's session was abnormal, and I hardly think coming close to dying is something you do every day."

I fell back onto the couch. "Fine. You have a point."

Logan sat by my side, the cushion dipping in his direction under his heavy weight. "Rest for an hour or two. If you're insistent on working more today, at least take a break first. You may feel up to healing again after you do."

It was on the tip of my tongue to tell him what I thought of his heavy-handedness when another wave of dizziness washed over me. I leaned more into the pillows. "Maybe I'll close my eyes for a little bit."

A satisfied grunt came from Logan before a soft blanket settled over me. Despite it being summertime, I pulled the blanket up higher and turned onto my side.

I'll just close my eyes for a few minutes, then I'll get back to work.

"DARIA? YOUR NEXT CLIENT IS HERE." Cecile's soft voice permeated my dream.

I snuggled deeper under the covers. I didn't want to wake. In my dream, Logan's hard warm arms surrounded me. Heat pressed against my back, and his body spooned me from behind.

When I opened my eyes, I fully expected to be alone on the couch and for the delicious dream to disappear. Instead, I became aware of the large male directly behind me, and my eyes widened.

I bolted upright. Logan's arm tightened around my waist, as if instinctively, before he loosened his grip. Embarrassment warmed my cheeks as I took in our position. On the small couch, he was actually spooning me, and our legs still lay entwined.

My mouth dropped. *What the hell?*

Logan wouldn't meet my gaze when I dragged my horrified expression to his. "I thought I went to sleep on the couch by myself?"

"You did," he replied, still avoiding eye contact.

Cecile crouched at my side and patted my hand. "You were having a nightmare and started thrashing. Logan tried to wake you, but you were sleeping too deeply, but as soon as he put his arms around you to stop your flailing, you calmed right down."

Logan pushed to a sitting position. Mussed hair covered his head, as if he'd run his hands through it repeatedly for the last few hours. My heart beat harder. He looked as sexy as hell, but he'd also been spooning me, and he had a girlfriend.

Heat flooded my cheeks.

"How do you feel?" he asked, his tone deep and warm, like butter melting over freshly baked bread.

"Fine," I replied in a clipped tone. "The nightmare must have been from Lucy's healing session."

Cecile cocked her head, her next words hesitant. "Your clients are waiting. Do you feel ready to perform?"

I pushed hair from my eyes and stood. The dizziness I'd felt earlier didn't return. I nodded vigorously. "Yeah, I'm fine. Just let me freshen up first."

I hurried to the back of the bus, my feet thumping softly on the floor. Once locked in the bathroom, I sank to the floor.

What in the holy hell just happened?

Logan had spooned me while I slept despite having a girlfriend.

The heat in my cheeks morphed from embarrassment to anger. *Just what kind of guy is he? That doing something like that is okay?*

Huffing, I stood and stepped to the sink. My irritated expression stared back at me in the mirror. After splashing cool water on my face, I combed my hair. My heart continued to pound, anger infusing adrenaline into me. Logan had spooned me, when I'd been *sleeping*. Granted, I didn't mind the feel of him against me, and Cecile had been watching over me, but . . .

I'd never slept next to another person before.

And the first time I'd done it, I'd been unaware of it, and I'd never consented to it. *And* he was my employee, *and* he had a girlfriend. Or, at least, I assumed he had a girlfriend.

Nothing about that situation was okay.

Yet . . .

I stopped combing my hair. If I were being *completely* honest with myself, I'd rather liked the feel of Logan against me, more than I wanted to admit.

I'd never felt another human's warmth and touch like that before, not since long ago when I was a little girl and my light had been immature and weak. The lack of that human connection, which all of us craved on some level, had left a gaping hole in my heart my entire life.

Yet Logan's touch, once again, hadn't bothered me. If anything, feeling him had been soothing, allowing me to rest.

I set the comb down. My turquoise eyes stared back at me as my forehead scrunched up. Still, I was Logan's boss.

And what would Crystal think if she heard her boyfriend spooned his employer just so she could sleep?

Yeah, I was pretty sure that would garner me the-least-liked-person-in-the-world status pretty quickly.

"Ugh."

Turning on stiff legs, I opened the door with a flourish and shrieked. Cecile stood in the doorway.

I brought a hand to my chest. "Cece! You scared me!"

She merely smiled.

I glanced behind her, but Logan had disappeared.

"He's outside, standing watch now that you're awake."

I leaned against the doorway, my chest still rising and falling quickly. "Did I really just take a nap with him? And did he seriously spoon me?"

Her eyes twinkled. "He's the one, Dar."

Obviously, *one* of us didn't see anything wrong with his actions. I rolled my eyes. "Cece, I'm his employer, and he has a *girlfriend*. He is most definitely not the one! And how can you think what he just did is okay?"

"Are you *sure* he has a girlfriend?"

"Yeah, her name's Crystal, and I'm pretty sure she'd bitch slap me if she knew I'd just spent the afternoon sleeping on the couch with her man."

"But the way he looks at you, I thought—"

I pushed past her. "Trust me. Don't think anything. It's what I've been trying *not* to do ever since I met him." I ducked to look out the window. "Is that a line by the magic shop?"

Cecile fluttered her hands. "You've been sleeping for two hours, and your clients have refused to leave and come back, so four of them are waiting. Let me go touch base with them. Stay here."

Cecile rushed out of the bus, and I approached the front hesitantly, peering down to peek through the windows again. Cecile had already reached my clients and was talking to them. The window near the front was open. Logan and his friends still stood watch.

Through the cracked opening, snippets of their conversation flowed in. I thought I heard my name.

I tiptoed closer, unable to help myself but stopped when I heard Logan's soft snarl.

"You know how I feel about that," Logan said quietly. "And Dar, she's . . . I don't know how to explain it. She's different. I've never met anyone like her."

My heart stopped, and I stood completely still.

"She does smell amazing," Alexander replied. "Like blooming roses."

Roses? I leaned down and sniffed my arm. *I don't smell like roses.*

"I get it," Brodie replied. "She's drop-dead gorgeous. I'll give you that, and fuck, those tits of hers."

Logan advanced on Brodie. "You'll keep your hands off her, and you won't talk about her like that." His voice dropped, taking on a strange cadence I hadn't heard before. Shivers ran down my spine.

KRISTA STREET

Brodie dipped his head, stepping back. "Whoa. Yeah, sorry, dude. I was just messing around. I didn't mean anything—"

A breeze cut off his words.

I stepped closer to the window to hear better. Logan's body had turned so stiff, I could have bounced a quarter off his shoulder, but at least he'd stopped advancing on Brodie.

Jake crossed his arms. "Even if she blows your mind, Loges, you know what's expected of you. And Crystal's your—"

A glass crashed to the floor when I bumped into the table.

Crap! I quickly picked it up, but when I looked back out the window, all four guys' attention had turned to the bus, their conversation stopping.

I ducked down, feeling like an idiot for hiding, but I didn't want them to know I'd been eavesdropping.

"Daria?" Cecile called, her voice coming through the cracked window. I peeked outside again. She walked across the pavement, away from the four clients waiting by the magic shop.

Double crap. So much for hearing anything else.

Logan and his friends parted as Cecile approached. She climbed up the stairs and smiled. "Are you ready?"

"Yeah, of course."

When I emerged from the bus, all eyes turned to me.

"You're up!" Alexander said cheerfully, his smile tight.

"And looking stunning, as always." Brodie winked.

"Sleep okay?" Jake asked.

Logan stood off to the side, his gaze averted.

"Yeah, but I have work to do." The tension strumming around the four of them was as thick as stew.

"We should get moving, Dar." Cecile bustled me toward the magic shop.

My attention returned to the task at hand, but hearing Logan say he'd never met anyone like me made my heart slam against my ribs. But what little I had heard of their conversation confirmed Crystal was Logan's girlfriend, or at least, someone meaningful to him which made his spooning me even worse.

Annoyance sparked within me again, but I took a deep breath and tried to focus on work. Clearing my throat, I said to Cece, "You weren't kidding about the line."

A small group of my clients congregated in the parking lot. I strode toward them. Logan automatically fell into step beside me, but he still wouldn't make eye contact.

I bristled.

He frowned, his heavy footsteps landing on the pavement. "Are you okay, Dar? Ready to work?"

"As ready as I'll ever be."

His frown grew. "Did you, uh, hear what we were talking about back there?"

I stopped so abruptly that I caught him off guard. He backpedaled until he stood in front of me. His warm chocolate irises gazed down at me, but his frown stayed in place.

"Yes, I heard. Something about Crystal, and me smelling like roses."

He sucked in a breath.

"And if it isn't bad enough that you spooned me while I was sleeping, it's even worse that you'd do that to your *girlfriend*."

His scowl deepened. "My girlfriend?"

"Yeah, you know, Crystal?"

His mouth parted, shock making his eyes widen.

But he didn't deny it. He didn't deny that Crystal was his girlfriend.

A million tons of disappointment fell down on me. I swung around, intent on returning to work, but Logan's hand shot out, stopping me mid-stride.

His warm fingers closed around my bicep. A thrill ran through me at the feel of him touching me again, and I wanted to kick myself for my reaction.

"Daria? Just what exactly did you hear?"

I brushed him off, pulling my arm away. "Nothing I didn't already suspect."

His jaw locked, and he opened his mouth again, but a fifth person rounded the corner and stepped up behind my waiting clients. Unlike the first four people in line, he appeared fine. He looked middle-aged and had dark-blond hair partially hidden by a baseball cap.

If I had seen him on the street, I would have assumed he was healthy.

Cecile gasped and grabbed my arm, her fingers digging into me and effectively ending my conversation with Logan, especially when my light seeped out of its storage box. Unlike with her usual touches, she didn't let go.

"What is it?" I asked.

The blood drained from Cecile's face as the fifth man began walking toward us. At the same time, Logan moved in front of me, protecting me, despite our second argument of the day.

"Cecile? What's wrong?" he asked in a deep voice.

She cleared her throat and pointed at the man approaching us. Her hand shook. "That . . . man." She licked her dry lips. "That man is Daria's father."

CHAPTER FOURTEEN

My eyes widened more with every step the man took.

I pulled away from Cecile, the zapping jolts from her touch becoming too much.

The man was only fifteen feet away, his swift pace bringing him closer to me by the second. I tried to see his features better, but Logan cut off my view.

My heart pounded. *My father is here? The man who left me when I was a baby? The man I wondered and dreamed about my entire life? He's actually here?*

Sweat erupted across my forehead, and I had the urge to fan my face. Logan reached around and lifted the back of his shirt. I gasped when his fingers curled around the gun peeking out of his waistband.

"Daria? Is that you?" the man called.

I peeked around Logan's shoulder. The man had

stopped two yards away. He was craning his neck, trying to see around my bodyguard.

I sidestepped Logan, getting a disapproving hiss from him.

"Yes," I said shakily. "I'm Daria." I brought a hand up to shade my eyes. The afternoon sun spilled onto the pavement, creating a glare. In the distance, my other four clients all fanned themselves in the heat.

The man removed his hat. "Your hair is blond, like mine."

My eyes narrowed as I took in his hopeful expression. Then, emotions welled up inside me like a tidal wave. Years of pain, loss, and the feeling that I hadn't been good enough poured into my response. "My hair is blond like my *mother's*."

He opened his mouth to respond, then seemed to think better of it.

Logan continued to hover in front of me, his body like a tensely coiled spring, ready to jump into action.

Blood pounded in my ears. If the man truly was my dad, I would never have known. He was of average height, had a broad nose, and a square jaw. Clad in jeans, a collared shirt, and a baseball cap, he looked like the average American dad. Yet he'd been anything but that. He had never been a father to me.

"You're all grown up." His expression turned sheepish. "You look just like your mother. I would have recognized you anywhere."

It was on the tip of my tongue to tell him that of course

I looked like my mom. My father could have had dark hair and dark skin, but those dominant genetics wouldn't have mattered—my magic wouldn't allow it. My skin still would have been pale, my eyes still turquoise, and my hair still flaxen blond. It was how the Gresham women's magic worked. We all looked the same regardless of our paternity.

But maybe my father had never known about my mother's magic.

He twisted his hat in his hands. "When I heard you were going to be in the area today, I . . . thought I'd come down and see you."

"How did you know—"

"Ms. Gresham?" An older man with stooped shoulders and a cane shuffled up behind my father. "My wife is getting very uncomfortable in this heat. Are you able to see her soon?"

I took a deep breath, forcing myself back into my healing role. "Of course, I'll be right there. Cecile? Can you help them inside?"

When Cecile stepped forward, my father dipped his head. "Cecile. It's been a long time."

She nodded stiffly, her expression guarded, before approaching the older gentleman. "If you'll come with me." She steered him away.

My heart pounded more since my father stood so close, but at the moment, I couldn't deal with that.

Too many conflicting emotions battled within me, making any further conversation impossible. The bottom line—he had abandoned me. Years of pain had followed his absence. He couldn't possibly think I would forget that he'd been a deadbeat and act as if nothing were amiss between us.

"I have to go." I stepped stiffly around Logan and past my dad.

My father's hand shot out, and I sucked in a breath when he grabbed my arm, but Logan intervened.

"Get your hands off her!"

A burst of energy from my father's touch shot through me. Painful shocks followed. He let me go when Logan advanced, but his pleading tone stopped me.

"Please. Please, Daria." He gave Logan a wary glance. "Just give me a chance. I'd like to speak to you. We've missed so much time together. Can I take you out for dinner tonight or a drink? I'd just like to talk to you. That's it."

Still reeling from the contact and my light's erratic response, I faced him squarely. With trembling movements, I crossed my arms over my chest. Part of me wanted to scream at him. Another part wanted to cry.

And one small part wanted to throw my arms around him and ask him why he'd left me.

Don't lose control, Dar. Not here.

I took a deep breath. "Why now? My entire life I was here, yet you left us. You left Mom and me, never to return. Why do you want to see me now?"

His hazel eyes softened. "I tried to find you earlier, but I couldn't. Your life was too transient. Trust me—if I could have found you, I would have."

My tensely crossed arms loosened. I let them fall to my sides. "How did you find me this time?"

"It's a small town. People talk. I heard you were coming here."

I glanced at Logan. A heavy frown marred his firm lips, and he still seemed ready to strike at any moment.

Shuffling my feet, I crossed my arms again. Nothing about my father was familiar, and everything about this encounter felt so weird, but my father was right. I'd lived like a nomad my entire life. It was plausible that if he'd tried to find me he wouldn't have been able to. *Maybe I should hear him out.*

I waved up the road. "There's a diner on the corner a few blocks that way. If you'd like, I'll meet you for dinner there at eight."

My father stopped twisting his baseball cap and grinned. "Eight o'clock, it is. I look forward to it."

IT WAS JUST past seven in the evening when I emerged from the bathroom. Since the rest of my healing sessions had gone relatively easily, I'd actually been able to take my time in the shower. Steam rolled into the hallway, fogging my view. If I wanted to blow-dry my hair before leaving I would have to hurry and—

"Oh!" I collided with a steel wall, or rather—Logan.

"Sorry." Logan faced me squarely in the narrow hallway. "I was pacing."

I waved away the steam that had temporarily blocked him from view. At least I was fully dressed in skinny jeans and a billowy short-sleeved top.

Logan's gaze flickered over my face. Jake, Alexander, Brodie, Cecile, and Mike all lounged at the front of the bus, giving Logan and me relative privacy since we were in the very back. From the tapping sounds coming from Alexander's fingers, I knew he was working on his laptop again. As of that afternoon, my stalker still hadn't clicked on any of the phishing links Alexander had sent.

I began towel-drying my hair. "Why were you pacing?"

Logan scowled and didn't seem to have any intention of telling me *why* he'd been waiting outside the bathroom.

"Is there something I can do for you?" My irritation over him spooning me that afternoon still hadn't worn off. If anything, the anxiety I felt over the upcoming dinner with my dad only strengthened it. Between the "present" I'd received that morning, my exhausting session with Lucy, and an impending dinner with my father, I was at my wit's end and couldn't handle any further arguments.

Logan's frown didn't lessen. "You're meeting him at eight?"

"That's right."

"Jake and I are going to sit two tables away from you. That's far enough to give you privacy but will also give me a clear view of what's happening and who's entering and exiting the building. Brodie and Alexander will be at another table, keeping watch. We've already staked out the restaurant. I'd like the hostess to seat you at a specific table."

I frowned and draped the towel on a rack in the bathroom, letting my damp hair trail down my back. "About that. I'd rather go there alone tonight."

Logan's eyebrows shot up. "Alone?"

"Yeah. Just me. It's only two blocks away, and I'll be with my dad in public. I'll be safe."

"Have you forgotten what happened this morning?"

A chill ran through me at the reminder. I crossed my arms tightly over my chest. "No. I haven't forgotten, but I don't want the four of you hovering around me in there. It will be hard enough as it is."

"What if we stay outside and keep watch?"

"Or what if you see me there safely, then give me some time alone to have dinner with my dad? I'll call you when we're done so you can walk me home."

His nostrils flared. "Not happening, Dar."

I bristled, my arms falling to my sides. "You know, last time I checked, I hired *you*." I poked a finger at his chest. His rock-hard muscle didn't soften, not even a little. "Which means I can tell you that I don't want your protection for one freakin' hour. I'll be in a public place with my dad. Even my crazy stalker wouldn't do anything in that circumstance. Considering how secretive he is and how he keeps covering his tracks, he obviously doesn't want to be caught. Showing up at a diner and cutting my head off probably isn't how he's envisioned killing me."

Logan's jaw clenched, the muscle in the corner pulsing. "Is this a game to you?"

"A game?" I scoffed. "Hardly. I'm taking this very seriously, actually, but tonight . . ." I tried to envision having dinner with my dad, having a conversation with him while four huge dudes hovered around me, distracting me at every turn. I swallowed tightly. "I just need to do this alone. I'm not stupid. I know my stalker is a threat, which is why I'd like you to escort me there and home. All I'm asking is to have dinner alone. That's it."

But Logan shook his head. "That's not how this works. You hired me to do a job. As a professional, I do the job until it's done which means I come with you and *stay* with you, whether you like it or not."

"And does that *'job'* of yours," I replied, putting air quotes around the word, "also require you sleeping by me?"

His mouth slackened.

"Cause doing *that* doesn't seem very professional to me." The words came out harsher than I intended them to, but whatever was going on between Logan and me was a mistake, a mistake I couldn't let happen, especially not when I was possibly facing the most important dinner of my life.

A moment of silence passed. Alexander's tapping continued in the background.

Finally, Logan lifted his chin, his eyes dark. "You're right. It wasn't professional. I won't do it again."

I swallowed and crossed my arms again, trying to tell myself that the hard look in his eyes didn't affect me. "As for tonight, I'm still doing this alone. Please, Logan. I want this dinner to be private."

The stormy expression on his face grew, but he replied in a clipped tone. "Understood." He turned, his shoulders tight, and walked stiffly back to the front of the bus.

I bit my lip, telling myself I hadn't done anything wrong by confronting him about my nap, but that angry expression on his face . . .

Sighing, I retreated to the bathroom, closing the door behind me. Steam still lingered, making my top dampen. I ignored it and grabbed the hair dryer, trying to concentrate on the task at hand, but a pit still formed in my stomach. A pit so big that it threatened to swallow me.

Shoving that feeling down, I plugged in the hair dryer and switched it on.

WE ARRIVED at the restaurant at quarter to eight—all five of us. Logan and his friends formed a protective circle around me on the sidewalk while we walked, as if my stalker could attack from any angle on the quiet small town street.

When we stepped into the diner's tiled entryway, I searched for my dad but didn't see him.

A young woman probably not much older than me stood behind the hostess counter with a bored expression on her face. Scents of grease filled the air.

"Five?" the hostess asked and grabbed five menus. Gum snapped in her mouth as she glanced appreciatively at Jake.

Jake gave her a crooked smile.

A fierce blush filled her cheeks.

"No, just one." I clutched my purse to my side, again searching the small diner for signs of my father.

"Oh." The hostess dropped four of the menus back onto the pile. "Yeah, sure. Whatevs. If you want to follow me."

Logan stepped closer to my side before saying under his breath, "We'll be heading out, but I want you to know that I don't like this, and I think I should stay."

I tightened my grip on my purse. "No. I want to be alone for this, but I'll call you when I'm done, and I won't leave the dining area. I'll make sure I'm always around people. I promise."

The tension rolling off Logan didn't lessen when he turned and stalked out the door. Brodie, Alexander, and Jake followed. Swallowing my anxiety about what was to come, I followed the hostess to a booth and slid into the seat.

"Specials are on the board up there." The hostess waved toward a chalkboard on the wall. "Your waitress will be with you in a sec."

She sauntered off, but instead of picking up my menu, I drummed my fingers on the table. According to my cell phone, it was still ten minutes to eight.

"Can I get you something to drink?" A waitress appeared with a pad in her hand. A white apron encircled her thick waist, and a little cap sat on her head, bobby pinned to her dyed-brown curls. All the place needed was a jukebox in the corner, and I would swear I'd just stepped back to 1950.

I shoved my cell phone back into my purse. "Um, a Coke is fine."

After jotting it down, she walked briskly back to the kitchen. Faint music from a radio somewhere in the back flowed through the air, and sizzling sounds came from the grill. A moment later, she plopped the Coke down in front of me.

"There ya go. Did you want to order?"

"No. I'm actually waiting for someone."

"Oh." She glanced at the lone menu in front of me. "I thought it was just you. I'll grab another menu."

The waitress returned a moment later with another menu just as the bell over the front door jingled. My father strolled in. He wore the same clothes as earlier, jeans and a collared shirt. When he saw me, he grinned.

My lips lifted into a tight smile, the butterflies in my stomach flapping their wings even more.

"I'm glad you came," he said when he slid into the seat across from me. The vinyl cushion squeaked until he got settled.

I fidgeted, and my knee moved up and down like a jack-hammer. "Um, yeah. No problem."

"You look nice."

I looked down at my billowy top. It was one of the nicer items of clothing I owned. "Thanks. So do you."

He chuckled. "Hardly. I just got off work and hurried

over. I wish I'd had a chance to shower and put more effort into it."

His easy smile made some of the nerves electrifying my stomach lessen. I picked up my menu. "Do you know what you want?"

"Oh, I'm not picky. A burger and fries will be fine. This place has great burgers."

When the waitress returned, I shoved my menu toward her after ordering the same as my dad then clasped my hands awkwardly under the table.

My father leaned forward. "You know, you've turned into a beautiful young woman. You look just like your mother was when I met her."

"She was beautiful, inside and out."

"Is she traveling with you now, or has she retired?"

I hastily took a drink of my fizzy Coke. "No. She, uh, she died in an accident last year."

His expression faltered. "Oh . . . I didn't know that."

As I set my drink down, bubbles from the Coke threatened to make me burp. "It was a car accident. She and Nan both died so now it's just me, Cecile, and Mike."

My father picked up a sugar packet from the condiment pile and played with it between his fingers, a troubled expression on his face. "I'm sorry to hear that. I wish I'd known."

I took another sip. Half of the soda was already gone in my nervous gulps. "Yeah. It was a, you know, hard time for all of us, but I still have Cecile and Mike."

His lips lifted, his smile filled with forced joy. "I remember Cecile, your mother's right-hand man."

"You mean woman?"

He laughed softly, effectively dispelling the somberness that had been forming.

The waitress returned with his drink and set the water down. "Food will be right up!" With that, she sailed off.

A moment of awkward silence passed between my father and me before I said, "Do you know that I don't even know your name?"

He stopped playing with the sugar packet. "My name's Dillon Parker. Didn't your mother tell you?"

I shook my head before saying hesitantly, "She never talked about you, and every time I asked, she said you weren't worth mentioning."

His lips turned down in a frown. "I guess that's to be expected."

Fiddling with my straw, I bit my lip, a million questions floating through my mind, but two in particular stood out. *Just ask him, Dar. You've always wanted to know, so now's your chance to learn the truth.*

I took a deep breath. "So . . . are you married? Do you have other kids?" I held my breath, too nervous to exhale.

He shook his head. "I never married, and I don't have any other kids—only you. I live alone here, just outside town."

I let out the breath I'd been holding. So I didn't have any brothers or sisters. Disappointment welled up inside me, but I pushed it down. *Don't stop now. Keep going before you lose your nerve.* I couldn't meet his eyes. "And . . . why did you leave us?"

He cleared his throat just as our food arrived.

"Here ya go." The waitress slid plates of steaming hot fries and greasy burgers on the table.

My dad tentatively picked up the ketchup before squeezing a large dollop by his fries. He frowned, an aggrieved expression filling his face before he finally replied, "Things weren't working out."

I waited for him to continue, but he didn't.

"So you just left? You didn't think about what that would do to me or Mom?"

He pushed a fry into his mouth, his jaw working fast. "I know you're probably angry with me, and you have every right to be, but your mother wasn't the easiest person to live with. I just couldn't stay."

My teeth clenched, even though his tone had been kind, not judgmental. "She was the best mother I could have ever had."

He nodded, although his earlier laidback demeanor had faded to a more uncomfortable one. But before I could ask more about his history with my mom, he hooked a thumb toward the window. "Do you know what's up with that guy staring at you through the window? He's been watching you this entire time."

I shifted uncomfortably, an image of my crazy stalker sitting just outside the diner watching me at that very moment running through my mind. Heart pounding, I hesitantly glanced toward the window.

Logan stood just outside.

Though I exhaled in relief, I inwardly cursed him for giving me the fright of my life. Glaring at him, I turned my attention back to my dad, only then realizing Logan had never left at all. He'd probably waited for my dad to arrive, staying back so I wouldn't see him, but then moved closer after my dad got settled. I gritted my teeth.

"Wasn't he with you this afternoon?" my dad asked, his tone turning worried.

"Yeah, he's actually my bodyguard."

His eyebrows shot up. "Why do you have a bodyguard?"

I forced myself to bite into a fry, but I swallowed it too quickly. The hot grease burned my throat, so I grabbed my Coke. "Because someone is threatening my life."

Shock filled my father's face. "Threatening your life? What the heck do you mean, Daria?"

"I mean that someone wants me dead." I eyed Logan. He still stood outside, making no attempts to hide himself. An image of the dead pigeon flashed through my mind.

"Jesus." My dad set his burger down. Ketchup oozed out from the sides. He leaned back in his seat, his food forgotten. "Who wants you dead?"

"I have no idea." I told him about the emails and their threats, but I left out the part about the dead pigeon on my doorstep.

"Have you gone to the police?"

I tensed. "No. No police."

"But you should call the police if someone wants to

hurt you. That's serious, Dar. They need to catch him and lock him up."

My insides stilled, my previous encounters with the police all too fresh in my mind. "No. I'm not calling the police. I won't call them."

"So instead of police, you hired a bodyguard?"

"You could say that."

He leaned forward, crossing his arms on the table. Worried hazel eyes met mine. "Why would someone want to kill you?"

"Your guess is as good as mine, but there's more than that. He also wants money." I sighed and pushed my plate away. Just the smell made me nauseous. "He said if I pay him fifty thousand dollars he'll let me live."

My dad's eyebrows shot up. "Then you should pay him. You don't need someone like that harassing you."

My jaw dropped. "Pay him? After he threatened to kill me?" I shoved my hands under the table, gripping them tightly together. "I'd never pay a prick like that. Besides, do you really think I have fifty thousand dollars lying around?"

An incredulous look filled his face. "How couldn't you? You're a famous healer, right?"

Exasperated, I shook my head. "I heal people because it's what I was meant to do. I don't get rich from it."

"Do you really expect me to believe that? I saw the line today. People were clamoring to see you. If you're not willing to go to the police, and you have a way to get rid of this guy, then you should. You need to stay safe, Daria. This sounds serious."

I gritted my teeth so hard that my jaw hurt. Annoyance flared through me that he was attempting to play the *dad card*. Even though I'd agreed to have dinner with him, that didn't mean I'd welcomed him back with open arms, and it certainly didn't give him the right to tell me what to do.

"That's not how it works. I only charge what people can afford. I don't do this for the money."

"But you could make that kind of money, couldn't you?"

Our waitress sauntered back to our table with the bill. She eyed my barely touched plate. "Do you want a box for that?"

"No. I've lost my appetite." I dug around in my purse for my wallet. A flush drifted up my neck. My own father thought I was rich, that I could easily pay my stalker off if I chose to. I snorted. Even he was naïve about how I lived.

My shoulders fell. *What did you expect?* The guy had abandoned me. He was no different from anyone walking by on the street. He didn't have the slightest clue about my life.

With a thick voice, I said, "I have to go."

My father caught my hand just as I shoved a ten-dollar bill on the table. My senses tingled. "You're leaving?"

I pulled my hand away. "I'm sorry. This was a mistake."

"Daria," my dad pleaded. "I'm sorry. I didn't mean to assume, and I didn't mean to tell you what to do. I can tell that I've upset you. Really, I'm sorry. Can we please see each other again? I don't want things to end like this."

As I studied his face, I couldn't tell if he was being genuine or not, but as much as I hated to admit it, I wanted him to care. I wanted that so badly. The little girl in me still existed, though I'd tried to stomp her into oblivion.

A part of me always longed for a dad, a man to swing me up in his arms, read me bedtime stories, and take me to the park after he got home from work. That little girl still lived deep within me despite my mother's refusal to talk about the man in front of me.

I swallowed the lump in my throat.

His eyes softened. "How about coffee in the morning? And I won't say anything else about the past or this stalker of yours. Let's just talk about the two of us. I still don't know anything about you, and I want to get to know you."

And I don't know anything about you. I nibbled my lip.

He laced his fingers together. Dirt lined his fingernails, as if he worked with his hands or didn't wash them frequently enough. With a start, I realized I didn't even know what he did for a job. "Please, Daria. I've only just found you."

Another moment passed before I finally replied, "Okay. I'll meet you for coffee tomorrow morning, but then I have to hit the road again, and I don't know—" I nibbled my lip again. "I don't know what the future holds for us."

But my father just grinned. "Great! I'll take whatever you're willing to give me, and there's a coffee joint up by the interstate. It's the only one, so you won't miss it. They make the best coffee around here."

I eyed my bodyguard. Logan still waited outside, his gaze unwavering.

Returning my attention to my father, I replied, "All right, fine. That works." Maybe the next day would go better.

"Excellent!"

A memory suddenly filled my mind, of being a little girl with my mom and my nan in a shopping mall. We'd just gone to the thrift store, hunting for clothes since I'd hit a growth spurt and had outgrown the stuff we'd bought a few months earlier. A girl around my age had been with her dad in the toy aisle. She'd had a shopping basket filled to the top with toys. Her father had been laughing, encouraging her to find more. Even though they were cheap toys, I still watched her. I never had an abundance of toys growing up. Even the dollar ones had been too expensive.

But that girl's father had showered her with gifts. It was the first time I understood what envy was.

"Daria? Is six too early?"

I snapped my attention back to my dad, the memory fading. "Sure. Six is fine."

CHAPTER FIFTEEN

"What did he say?" Logan asked the second I stepped out of the diner.

Wind whipped down the street, blowing my hair. "You seriously have the guts to ask me that after you stayed when I specifically asked you to leave?"

He scowled. "It's my job to protect you. There was no way I was leaving you here alone."

I rolled my eyes and took off down the street. Logan fell into step beside me. Our feet tapped on the pavement as I gripped my purse tighter.

The dinner still played over in my mind like a spinning record that wouldn't stop. My father and I had parted ways awkwardly at our table. I'd had the ridiculous urge to hold out my hand for a handshake, as if we'd just conducted a business meeting, but of course, I didn't. I never touched if I could avoid it, but my father didn't know that.

He'd pulled me into a hug, causing my senses to flare to life, but the hug was so brief, my healing light stayed buried in my storage chest. However, his contact was enough for his scent to linger on my shirt. A trace of cigarette smoke had been in his clothes along with a hint of alcohol on his breath. The latter surprised me, as he'd seemed perfectly sober.

"Why are you frowning?"

I nearly tripped over a crack in the sidewalk. "I'm frowning?"

Logan's stormy gaze hadn't lessened. "Yeah, and you looked upset a few times while you were having dinner."

"Well . . . wouldn't you be if your parent abandoned you?"

He had the decency to look sheepish. "Did he say anything about why he left?"

"He said things weren't working out, and that my mom wasn't easy to live with, but that was about it. Our food arrived when that conversation started." *Then it shifted to him encouraging me to pay off my stalker.* I leaped off the curb and onto the street at an intersection. A part of me wanted to run, anything to not think about how upsetting the dinner with my dad had been, but just when I picked up my pace, Logan pulled me across the street to the other side, away from where my tour bus waited.

I startled at the feel of him touching me. "Logan? What are you doing?"

A truck rounded the corner farther down the street. A heavy plume of diesel smoke filled the air when it passed.

A frown settled on Logan's face, his eyebrows drawing tightly together. "You're upset, and I don't like that." He said the last part quietly, almost too quietly for me to hear, before he headed up the sidewalk toward a fast food restaurant, me in tow.

"So, we're going to a fast food restaurant?"

"Yeah. You barely touched your food back there. You need to eat."

Even though a part of me wanted to lash out at him for his heavy-handedness, deep down, I knew it was only because I wanted to forget everything about my dad. Taking it out on Logan wouldn't help.

The scent of grease assaulted me when we stepped inside the burger joint. I bit my lip and studied the menu, but all the words seemed to jumble together.

Logan scanned the menu, too, his broad shoulders straining against his T-shirt. "Anything look good?"

"Um . . ." I picked the first picture I saw. "A chicken sandwich is fine." I pulled out my wallet and grimaced at the meager bills inside.

"That's it?" Logan's gaze drifted to my wallet. He stepped to the counter and pulled out his billfold before saying to the checkout girl, "Two chicken sandwiches, two large fries, and two strawberry milkshakes."

"Logan, you don't have to do that. I can pay for myself."

He didn't even glance at me when he pulled out a twenty.

A rush of gratitude ran through me when I stuffed my wallet back in my purse. Money was always tight for

Cecile, Mike, and me. I snorted quietly. Too bad my dad didn't understand that.

When our food was ready, Logan picked up the tray.

"Thank you," I said, keeping my gaze down. "For buying me dinner."

"Not a problem. Where do you want to sit?"

"By the window?"

We settled into a small booth overlooking the street. A few cars drove by, headlights on, as the sky darkened. My stomach growled when I picked up my sandwich, reminding me I really *hadn't* eaten dinner.

Logan's jaw worked rhythmically as he chewed a fry. Tense energy that hadn't been there earlier surrounded him.

I ducked my head and slurped from the milkshake. A strawberry sucked into my mouth, the flavors coating my tongue. Logan continued to eat, his dark gaze fluttering across my face every now and then, but every time I tried to make eye contact, he would look away. For the life of me, I couldn't decipher what he was thinking.

"Should we go?" I asked ten minutes later. Logan had just polished off his last fry so I picked up my milkshake. "I can drink this on the way back."

Logan wiped his mouth on a napkin and took our tray to the garbage. Once we were outside, I sucked my milkshake self-consciously. That tension hadn't left Logan's shoulders, and he kept giving me sideways glances.

Our feet tapped on the pavement, and wind rustled through the boulevard's trees. I was acutely aware of how closely he walked at my side. Since nighttime had fully set in, the traffic had died down, and nobody else strolled on the sidewalk. We had at least another three blocks before we reached the bus, and with the quietness that surrounded us, it felt as if only he and I existed in the tiny town.

"Do you want to talk about anything that happened at the diner?" Logan asked abruptly.

I nibbled my lip and finished my shake. When we crossed the street, I tossed it into the first trash bin I saw.

"You just looked so upset, and I, uh . . ." He raked a hand through his hair. "If you want to talk about it, I'm happy to listen."

I peeked up at him, remembering our conversation on the hill overlooking the rest stop and how he'd listened then too. A breeze ruffled my hair, carrying with it faint scents from the fast food joint.

"I thought he'd be different," I finally replied.

"Go on."

My heart rate picked up. Nervously, I threaded my fingers through my long blond hair. All of a sudden, I felt unsure if I was still mad at Logan about the nap and dinner, or if in the grand scheme of life, none of that really mattered compared to repairing a relationship with the only blood family member I had left. So many things had happened since the morning and all at once. I groaned inwardly. I truly didn't even know how I felt about anything anymore.

I sighed.

"Talking might help." The storm still filled Logan's eyes, but something else did, too—worry.

"Do you really want to hear about it?"

"Yeah. I do," he replied quietly. "It was obvious your dad upset you, and I know that talking about stuff can help you."

My breath stopped. In all of my twenty-one years, I'd never had someone to talk to about my dad. Since my mom refused to discuss him, and since Mike and Cecile didn't feel it was their place to mention him, I was left with only my imagination to determine what he'd been like.

Once again, Logan was offering to fill a void in my life, just as he had done on the hill over looking the rest area. He was actually willing to be there for me to talk about the important things, the *really* important things, when no one else would.

Something inside me warmed and softened. My earlier anger over the nap and dinner suddenly seemed trivial.

"I just thought," I finally said, "that he'd be *more*." I slowed my pace, and Logan adjusted his stride to match mine. "When I was little, I imagined he might be a secret government spy who worked abroad and couldn't come to me because it would put me in danger, or that he was a great explorer and had too many obligations to better humanity's quest for knowledge, which kept him away." The tightness in my chest returned. "They were childish fantasies. Things I made up so I wouldn't feel like there was something wrong with me—that *I* wasn't the reason he left—but as I got older, I knew none of those excuses could be true."

A breeze whistled through the trees, fluttering my hair in front of my eyes. I pushed it back, my hands trembling.

Logan's dark, steady gaze continued to bore into me. He nodded encouragingly.

After taking another deep breath, I said, "When I was a teenager, I thought maybe he'd married someone else and had other kids, and the reason he never found me was because his new wife didn't want him living in the past, but I never pictured him living in a small town by himself with no children."

Logan frowned. "I imagine most kids make up stories about parents that abandon them. It's easier to believe something happened to that parent, something that didn't allow the person to be a part of their child's life, than to accept that the person abandoned them on purpose."

My throat tightened. "Exactly. I've known for a long time that he chose to leave me. He's not a secret government spy, and he's not even married." I shrugged, tears threatening to pool in my eyes. I hastily blinked them back. "But it sucks, you know? Even though I've spent my life traveling, I still saw other kids with their dads. Playing with them or teaching them how to ride their bikes." I laughed, the sound slightly hysterical. "The ironic thing is that I don't even know how to ride a bike. We could never afford one."

A deep groove appeared between Logan's eyes, that heavy scowl flashing across his face again. "He's the one who lost out by leaving you. You're a good person, Daria. I haven't known you long, but I've seen enough to know that."

My heart beat harder at his quiet admission. I hastily looked away. "Do you know I thought I'd recognize him if I ever saw him? Like, I'd feel something or just *know* that he was my dad? But nothing like that happened. If Cecile hadn't pointed him out this afternoon, I wouldn't have looked at him twice, and I know he said he couldn't find me before despite trying, but . . . I don't know. Surely, if he wanted to be in my life, he would have found a way."

A faint glow rimmed Logan's irises, but then he blinked and it was gone.

I frowned, once again wondering if I was seeing things.

"And how are you feeling about him now?" he asked.

Shaking myself, I replied, "I'd be lying if I said I wasn't hurt. For the past few years, I haven't thought about him much, and I thought I was over never having a dad, but then meeting him today . . ." I shook my head. "It's all rushing back. I guess the little girl in me still hopes her dad will come home and sweep her off her feet one day. Maybe the reality isn't quite what I imagined, but he does want to see me again."

"Do you want him in your life?"

"I don't know. A part of me does, but the other part of me still feels . . ." I scrunched my nose, trying to identify the feeling.

"Betrayed?"

"Yes," I breathed. "That's exactly how I feel."

A lone car drove past on the quiet street, several people in the back seat laughing and talking through the open windows. I glanced toward them, grateful for the distraction. The intensity of our conversation threatened to clutter my thoughts, and I was having a hard time remembering that Logan had a girlfriend.

I nodded toward the car. "Looks like someone's having a good night."

Logan abruptly stopped, just outside an old record shop. The vintage store looked original, as most of the shops in the town did, as though we'd stepped back into another era. He glanced at the retreating vehicle. "I think there's a bar up the road. I saw it when we drove in."

I wrapped my arms around myself, warding off the cooling temperature. Logan stepped closer, his heat drifting my way. My body hummed, desire fluttering in my belly.

Despite desperately trying to recall why I couldn't let anything happen between us, I said, "Thank you. For listening again."

Logan stuffed his hands into his pockets. "It's fine. I like listening to you."

He stood so close, closer than he ever had before. If I stepped forward just one small step, my breasts would brush against his chest.

My chin dropped, my breath coming faster. With him so near, his scent fluttered to me—sandalwood and forest. Crap, he smelled good. I closed my eyes.

Don't do it, Dar. Don't! He has a girlfriend. He's your

employee. He freakin' slept beside you this afternoon and you barely know him. You're playing with fire.

But Logan was the one to move. Not me. He took a step closer, and my boobs grazed his chest.

I stopped breathing and tilted my head up. A subtle glow lit his irises, and this time I felt certain I wasn't imagining it, but before I could comment, his head dipped, his lids growing hooded.

His lips drifted closer to mine, his sweet breath beckoning me. I leaned forward, my lips only millimeters away from his. A low growl filled his chest, making my insides purr.

"Hey, lovebirds!" Another car whizzed past us, a crowd of drunken college kids in the back. One hung out the window and whistled a long catcall.

My eyes widened, and I jumped away from Logan. Mortification filled me. What the hell was I doing? Had I almost just *kissed* him? I ruffled a hand through my hair, nervous tingles shooting along my skin, making goose bumps erupt.

Logan grumbled something under his breath as the car sped away.

I cursed inwardly, my breath still coming so fast that a moment of dizziness washed through me. What was I doing? No, what were *we* doing?

I'd almost just kissed him, but it didn't change things. Logan was with Crystal, and he was my employee. Nothing about this was okay.

Fuck me, and the horse I rode in on.

My stomach tightened as disgust with myself rose in my throat like thick bile. "We should head back."

Logan's jaw locked, his voice tight. "Yeah, of course."

I turned and took off at a rapid walk. Logan followed. For a large man, his steps were surprisingly quiet, but I still sensed him. Hell, my body practically vibrated for him, as if every cell hummed and responded to his presence.

The distance to the bus passed in a tensed, awkward blur. I kept well away from Logan, even walked ahead of him a few times just so it would make talking awkward.

When we reached the bus, Jake and Brodie sat on the couch beside Alexander, who had his laptop open, his fingers flying across the keyboard. The three of them all wore tense expressions.

Cecile and Mike sat at the kitchen table playing a game of cards.

Brodie lifted his chin. "Glad you made it back."

Jake merely cocked his head, his expression curious as he gazed at Logan and me, while Alexander continued tapping away.

"You didn't want us to walk back with you?" Jake asked.

Logan's fingers curled into his palms. "Something came up."

He didn't elaborate, but all three of his friends looked my way.

"Have there been any more emails from my stalker?" I asked, anything to change the subject as I dropped my purse by the door.

Alexander shook his head, his dark hair grazing the top

of his glasses. "No. I'm sending a few more phishing emails, but if that doesn't work, I'll try something else."

"Have you found anything else about him?" Logan asked.

Logan brushed past me, his entire body like a hot, stiff board. Maybe I was imagining things, but he seemed as shaken up by what had almost transpired between us as I was.

He settled down beside Alexander without looking at me again, but I still noticed his clenched jaw and felt the unspent energy rolling off him like a tightly coiled spring just waiting to launch.

I walked past all of them, my stomach fluttering for multiple reasons. Something was growing between Logan and me—that much was obvious—but it spelled bad news. The reality was that sooner or later, we would discover who my stalker was and deal with it, then Logan would be on his way, returning to his everyday life, a life that didn't include me and most likely included Crystal.

Cecile's expression grew more and more worried as I approached her. I could only imagine what I looked like. It had been a long freakin' day.

"Did it go okay with your dad?" She stood from the table when I reached it, her frown growing.

"As well as it could, I guess. We didn't talk long." I bit my lip, remembering my dad's advice to pay off my stalker. "I'm meeting him again in the morning before we go. Just one last time to say goodbye."

Mike's eyebrows rose in surprise. "Is that what you want?"

I shrugged. "Honestly, I'm not really sure what I want, but I'm open to seeing him again."

Cecile squeezed my hand but let go just as the storage chest I buried my light in cracked open. With her touch gone, my light settled back down. "Whatever you want to do, honey. We're behind you one hundred percent, but you know that."

I smiled gratefully. "I know. Thank you."

Mike pulled his Yankees cap off and set it on the table, clearing his throat. "We just want you to be happy, Dar."

Cecile nodded. "But you look exhausted, honey. You should go on to bed."

I nodded but my attention drifted back to Logan. He was deep in conversation with Alexander as both of them stared at the computer screen. I debated returning to the front of the bus, realizing I'd never told Logan my plans for the morning, but his frown stopped me. Whatever he and Alexander were discussing appeared intense. And honestly, the thought of interacting with him again made me so anxious that I wanted to throw up.

Besides, it was just my dad, and for once, I wanted to have a private conversation with him—a truly *private* conversation.

My forehead scrunched up as I remembered the dead pigeon. *Is that really a good idea, Dar? Going completely alone?*

But if I wanted to truly be alone with my dad, there was

only one way to guarantee it. I'd have to sneak out in the morning to see him before we left and not let Logan know.

The only comfort I took was in the fact that the end of the month hadn't arrived. According to my stalker, my deadline to pay him wasn't until then, so supposedly, I didn't have to actually worry about him hurting me for another week.

Still, I would need to be careful. If he'd found me at the rest stop, that meant he could possibly find me again.

A shiver ran through me, and I wondered if the risk was truly worth it, but then I pictured my dad, and the aching hope of finally having the father I'd always dreamed of welled up in me again.

I was willing to take that chance.

CHAPTER SIXTEEN

S oft snores filled the bus when I woke the next morning, my vibrating alarm waking me from a tormented sleep. Dreams had plagued me all night. In a way, it felt as if I hadn't slept at all.

The hour was early, just after five o'clock. Not even the sun had risen.

I pushed the covers back and hopped down silently from my bunk. People lay sleeping all around. I hurried to the bathroom, threw clothes on, and twirled my hair up into a ponytail.

When I emerged, my gaze drifted to Logan. He slept soundly, his chest rising and falling deeply with each breath. I wasn't surprised by his exhausted sleep. He and Alexander had been up late. I'd woken at two in the morning to see both of them still hovering around Alexander's computer before I'd turned on my side and drifted back to another fitful rest.

I scurried to the front of the bus, my steps as quiet as a mouse's. With any luck, I would be back before Logan woke which meant I wouldn't have to deal with his wrath for sneaking out. I didn't plan to spend more than half an hour at the coffee shop anyway since I had a show that afternoon which meant I needed to focus.

After stepping over Jake's long legs, which sprawled into the aisle, I reached the front of the bus and exited as quietly as I could.

I surveyed the ground, half expecting another headless bird to greet me, but all that waited was clean pavement.

"Thank God," I whispered, not realizing until that moment how worried I'd been about another unexpected "present" from my stalker.

Cool morning air washed across my cheeks outside. I continually looked over my shoulders, assessing for anybody lurking about or any parked cars with shadowed outlines in them.

But nobody was around. The quiet town continued to sleep, none the wiser that someone wanted me dead.

I took off, knowing the longer I lingered by the bus, the more likely it was my bodyguards would notice my absence. Walking toward the main street, I pulled out my phone and searched for a hired ride. According to my map app, only one coffee shop was by the interstate. It wouldn't be hard to find.

A few minutes later, a car pulled up, and I hopped in with relief. I was officially around somebody in public.

"Where to?" the driver, a middle-aged man with a mustache, asked.

But then I eyed him warily, my relief vanishing. Who's to say he wasn't my stalker?

"Um . . . the coffee shop by the interstate. Do you know which one?"

He flashed me a tired grin in the rearview mirror. "Sure do. There's only one."

His smile looked genuine, and he pulled the car out, driving toward the interstate in the direction of the coffee house at a normal speed. My shoulders sagged. He'd probably been working through the night driving around those drunk college kids, and he was nothing more than a random hired driver.

Ten minutes later, he dropped me off. Noise from the nearby interstate filled the air. Even at this early hour, vehicles flew past.

Across the road lay a truck stop and a McDonald's. Tired travelers filled their cars with gas, and truckers ate breakfast inside the fast food joint. Plenty of people lingered about despite the early hour. My anxiety lessened, and I stopped gripping my phone so tightly in my pocket.

A bell on the door jingled when I stepped inside the cafe, and scents of coffee assaulted me. A lone barista stood behind the counter, wiping it down. Since the hours on the window said they opened at five thirty, I guessed she was still setting up.

I searched around for my dad but didn't see him. It

wasn't quite six yet, so I figured I'd beaten him. Fiddling with my ponytail, I approached the counter.

The young barista smiled. "What can I get you?"

I picked the cheapest thing on the menu. "A small black coffee is fine. Can you make it to go?" I checked the time again. I would have to leave by half past six. Hopefully, my dad would show up soon.

After paying for and getting my drink, I sat at one of the tables. The chair wobbled when I pulled it out. One leg was shorter than the others so it kept teetering as I waited on the edge of my seat. Literally.

I checked the time again as a car pulled up to the drive-thru. Behind the counter, the barista got to work. Machines hissed and fresh scents of coffee filled the air, but even those inviting sounds and smells didn't ease the pit forming in my stomach.

The clock read ten after six, and a sickening sense of doom that my father had stood me up began to settle in.

"Miss?" The barista leaned over the counter, waving a phone. "Are you Daria?"

I jerked upright so quickly that I almost dropped my coffee. "Um . . . yes. That's me."

"You have a phone call." She waved the phone again. "Can you make it quick? We usually get a lot of phone orders at this time from people heading to work and wanting to bring in drinks."

I stumbled when the teetering chair caught on the floor. "Yeah. Sure. Um, thanks."

She handed me the phone, and I brought it tentatively to my ear. "Hello?"

"Daria? Is that you?"

Even though I'd just met him, I recognized my dad's voice. "Yeah. It's me. Where are you?"

"I'm sorry. My alarm didn't go off, and since I don't have your number, I had no way to call you. I'm glad I was able to reach you at the coffee house."

My stomach sank. *He's canceling.* "No, it's fine. I should get back to the bus, anyway."

"No, no! I still want to see you. Is there any chance you can come to my place before I go to work? I'd really like to see you before you leave, and the coffee shop is on the opposite side of town from where I work. I need to shower quickly, but I should be out by the time you get here."

"Um . . ." *Go to his house alone?* It was one thing to meet my dad in a public place but another entirely to go to his home. Logan would be royally pissed off if I did that. "I can't. I need to get back."

"Please, Daria. I really want to see you. I'd like to be in your life again if you're willing, and I also have something of your mother's. I want to make sure I get it to you before you leave."

"Something of Mom's? What is it?"

"A ring that her mother, your grandmother, gave her. She lost it when we were together. She said something about it being in your family for generations. I found it a few years ago, buried in an old shoebox. It must have fallen in there somehow."

My breath stopped. I knew exactly what he was talking about. My mom had mentioned the ring before—a family heirloom that the Gresham women treasured. "What does it look like?"

He paused, as if rummaging through the shoebox before pulling it out. "It has a large emerald in the center and a swirly pattern on the band."

My chest tightened. *That's it!* A sense of elation filled me. My mom would have been so happy to have that ring back. I closed my eyes, tears filling them. In a way, it felt as though I'd just regained a small part of my mother. That ring had meant so much to her.

I blinked back the tears.

The barista looked at me expectantly, and I remembered her request to not take too long on the phone. "Okay, I'll come. Where do you live?"

He rattled off his address, and I hung up.

"Thanks." I handed the phone back to her. As soon as the barista hung it up, it rang again. She answered and began taking an order.

I pulled out my phone, my fingers shaking in anticipation, and sent a quick text to Cecile.

> Morning, Cece. My dad's alarm didn't go off, so he missed coming to the coffee shop. I'm taking a car to his house right now. He said he has Mom's ring! Can you believe it? I'll be quick, so I'll be back soon. And if Logan wakes up, can you cover for me?

At the last moment, I tapped in my dad's address at the end. Better to let Cecile know where I was in case they needed to pick me up if I couldn't get another ride. I cringed. Logan would be livid if that happened.

After sending the text, I searched for another ride. Between the coffee and hired cars, my funds were dwindling, but a chance at finding my family's lost ring and knowing that my dad and I could be kindling a new relationship made being broke worth it.

When the new driver finally pulled up, I slid into the back, a grin on my face, and gave him my dad's address. My stomach flipped the entire way as he drove north of town. The small city fell behind us as wilderness grew.

"Do a lot of people live out here?" I asked the driver. Pine trees flashed by my window, and we'd driven at least five miles out of town.

He shook his head. "Not many. Just a few cabins here and there."

Gravel crunched under the tires when he pulled onto a driveway off the narrow highway. An old mailbox teetered on its edge. I frowned as I took in the neglected property.

"Here you go." He pulled up to an old trailer home. It looked decrepit and rotten, as if a strong wind could push it over.

My hand lingered on the door handle as I once again considered how much Logan would hate what I was doing. *But you sent Cecile that text. They know where you are, and you're about to get Mom's ring back—you'll actually have a part of her again.*

Still . . .

I eyed the driver in his mirror. "Do you mind waiting to give me a ride back?"

The driver checked his watch. "I can wait as long as I don't get another call. Will you be long?"

"No, I won't be long. I just need to say goodbye to someone and grab something. Five to ten minutes max. Is that okay?"

He sighed. "Fine, but make it quick."

I hurried out the door. Thick woods surrounded the property. Forest scents filtered through the air along with the smell of gasoline, and an old generator hummed somewhere.

Rickety porch steps swayed beneath my feet when I climbed up to the mobile home. I knocked once on the door, and my father immediately opened it. He smiled and stepped to the side. "Thanks for stopping by." He eyed the vehicle behind me. "Come on in."

Cigarette smoke lingered in the air when I stepped into the dingy trailer. Next came the appalling realization of how my father lived. Dirty dishes lined the counter in the old kitchen. Soiled clothes lay in a pile on the saggy couch, and a hint of body odor wafted from my father.

My nose wrinkled. I couldn't help it. "I can't stay long." I wrapped my arms around my middle. "We're leaving town soon." When I turned around to face my dad, my head cocked. "I thought you said you had to shower."

Greasy hair lined his head. I took a step back and put my hand in my pocket, comforted that my phone was so close. A pit formed in my stomach as I studied my dad's appearance. He definitely hadn't showered despite claiming that was what he would be doing.

I looked around for the ring, in his hand or on the counter but saw no sign of it.

Something's not right here . . .

"Dad?" I asked uneasily, startled that I'd just called him *dad* for the first time.

But instead of responding, my dad sidestepped me and was out the front door before I could stop him. He waved to the driver.

Jaw dropping, I realized he was waving the driver off. I bolted out the door behind him. "No! I need him to give me a ride back!" The queasy feeling in my stomach grew as red taillights disappeared up the drive.

Warning alarms went off inside me. Something was definitely wrong. Something was very, very wrong.

Run, Dar! Run now!

A survival instinct roared to life, and I barreled forward as my father turned back to me, his gaze hard.

I pushed past him, not questioning the instinct screaming at me to run, but in a frighteningly fast move, my father grabbed my upper arm just as I tried to take off down the porch stairs.

His fingers squeezed my bicep as he wrenched me back inside. I yelped and tried to break free, but his grip was too strong.

"Let me go!" I fought wildly, thrashing and kicking. *Shit!*

My mind reeled as my light flew out of my storage chest. Sensations jolted through me.

I thrashed harder, doing everything I could to break free.

But I couldn't.

My father shoved me back inside and slammed the door behind him before he pushed me to the floor. I scrambled back, blubbering pleas coming from me. "No! Please, no! Please don't do this!"

My father smiled, the sight chilling. "Tick tock. Tick tock."

My insides froze, the familiar words turning my blood to ice. I scampered back on the floor, my heart pounding as horror swirled through my veins.

Terror swallowed me whole as I stared up into the eyes of my father—the stalker who wanted to kill me.

CHAPTER SEVENTEEN

"It's you! You're the one who's been threatening me!"

He leered before clapping in a mocking way. "Very good. You're finally catching on."

"But . . . what about the ring?" I scrambled back more on the dirty carpet and pushed to stand. My thighs backed into an end table. My father stood only feet away, but I couldn't retreat any farther.

He engaged the lock on the front door. The sound of that bolt sliding into place made my stomach heave. He gave me a chilling smile. "There is no ring, and I need money."

"No ring?" It was all I could manage before words from his email floated to the front of my mind. *Since you haven't paid, the day is coming . . .*

"But I had until the end of the month!"

"Not anymore. I need the money now, or they're coming after me."

"Who's coming after you?" It occurred to me the longer I kept him talking, the better chance I had of finding a way to escape.

"I owe some guys some money."

My mind whirled. No wonder he'd encouraged me to pay off my stalker the previous night. He'd wanted me to pay *him*. And when I'd refuted his argument, he'd set up another meeting for us—a meeting where he got me alone. My mom had obviously told him about the ring—that was how he knew about it, and he probably knew I desperately wanted it back.

I'd fallen right into his trap.

Shit! Shit! Shit! My thoughts somersaulted as I realized how foolish I'd been. I discreetly felt for my phone. If I could get a quick call to Logan and keep my phone hidden, he would be able to hear what was going on.

I subtly pulled my phone out of my back pocket and kept it hidden behind my thigh while asking my father more babbling questions. Peeking down as evasively as possible, I pulled up Logan's number. I was pushing the green button when my father's eyes widened. His hand flew forward and snatched my phone away.

"What the hell are you doing?" he snarled.

I lunged forward, trying to grab it. From out of nowhere, his hand sailed from the right and smacked my cheek so hard that my head spun.

"You little bitch! Who are you trying to call?"

His chilling words and the ringing in my ears had terror sliding through my veins. He grabbed me, his hands digging painfully into my arms. "Who knows you're here?"

I yelped.

"Who? Dammit! Tell me!"

"No one," I lied. I could only pray that Cecile had read my text and would come for me. I sent up a silent prayer of thanks that I'd given her my dad's address.

My father shook me again, bringing my attention back to him. "You're going to get me the money now! Move!"

He shoved me toward the back of the trailer. I dug my heels in, but it didn't help. He lifted me off the ground and threw me forward.

I sailed through the air for a split second before my head cracked into the wall. My vision threatened to go dark.

I muttered a spell under my breath, breaking my rule of never practicing my telekinetic magic in front of others. A lamp flew off the table in the direction of my father, but he ducked just in time.

I had another spell halfway done when he slammed his foot into my stomach, kicking me so hard I couldn't breathe, let alone cast a spell.

"You're just like your mother! A filthy witch! What you two do is an abomination!"

Tears filled my eyes at his cruel words. I pushed against the wall, my movements clumsy as I tried to stand while oxygen refused to enter my lungs. *I can't breathe!*

My father loomed above me, any trace of the caring

man I'd met the previous evening gone. Something warm and sticky dripped into my eye. I brought my hand to my forehead. It came away dripping with blood.

Genuine tears filled my eyes then as I stared up at the man who'd no doubt abused my mother. Everything became crystal clear—her unwillingness to talk about him, the way she tensed up whenever I mentioned him.

I'm sorry, Mom. I didn't know. If I'd known, I never would have agreed to meet him.

"Get up!" My father seethed.

A hook in the wall poked into my back. I scrambled to stand, but I swayed again, probably from lack of oxygen to my brain. Pitiful hoarse gasps emitted from my mouth.

The second I was on my feet, he shoved me toward the back of the trailer. Despite the blood trailing down my face and the dizziness, I frantically searched for a way out. *No windows in the hall. There's a front door behind us. There! In the corner! There's a window there!*

My dad abruptly latched onto my arm, as if sensing I was about to hurtle out the window. My light flowed forth again at the feel of his hand on me, its strength making me want to barf.

He wrenched my mouth open and stuffed a rag in, effectively stopping any chance I had at using magic around him again.

I gagged against the cottony filth, the taste making my stomach heave.

"You're going to pay me now."

"But I don't have any money!" I mumbled through the

rag, my words barely coherent. I dragged in another breath through my nose, some oxygen flooding my lungs.

"I know, but that doesn't mean you can't get it. You're going to contact every one of your upcoming clients and demand that they each pay you five thousand dollars if they want to be seen. You'll tell them to deposit the money into the account I give you, and they have one hour to do it. Do it now! If at least fifty thousand dollars isn't in my account within the hour, you die."

He pushed me forward, his grip still firm. Electric shocks continued to travel down my arms.

A desk sat in the corner of the back bedroom. It held a computer with two screens and other pieces of tech. Dirty clothes, empty beer bottles, and takeout boxes littered the floor. He pointed at the laptop. "Pull their phone numbers up from their emails."

He knows their contact information is in my email? I stumbled on the carpet but stayed upright. He shoved me toward the computer.

A part of me still couldn't believe what was happening. My own father, the man I'd dreamed about my entire life had probably abused my mother and was most likely going to kill me after he got his money, but the pain that evoked was quickly smothered with another emotion.

"No!" I yelled through the rag, refusing to sit at the computer as anger swirled in my gut.

He raised his hand to hit me again, but I ducked just as he swung.

"Bitch!"

I used the momentum of his failed attack to my advantage. Bending low, I shouldered him in the gut. He let out a loud *oomph* before falling back. I didn't slow even though I had a hard time staying on my feet. I ripped the dirty rag from my mouth, rushed past him, and raced for the door.

At the last second, his hand shot out and grabbed my ankle. I fell forward just as my eyes alighted on an unbelievable sight through the living room window.

As I hit the ground, a large black wolf crashed through the glass, the ear-splitting sound filling the house.

I landed on the ground, hard, the wind knocked out of me. My lips parted as my heart beat so painfully I thought it would explode.

"What the hell?" my father said.

The huge wolf didn't stop. The second it landed on the grimy living room carpet, it ran at full speed straight toward us. Broken glass clung to its black fur, but its eyes glowed as they locked onto my father.

Taking shallow, stifled breaths, I shrank back against the wall as howls from outside reached my ears. The wolf leaped over me and headed straight for my dad, snarling. Pitiful cries from my dad came next.

Just as quickly, another wolf jumped through the broken living room window, that one a dark-gray color.

Then two more wolves jumped through, just behind the dark-gray one. The three advanced, each of them running toward the black wolf, who held my father pinned to the floor, his huge jaws clamped around my father's neck.

"Holy shit!" I whispered as trembles wracked my body. I

sat completely still against the wall, too terrified to move. *Is this really happening?*

The gray wolf, and the other two—both dark gray with streaks of white and cream—circled my father and the first wolf.

My mind reeled with the unbelievable situation that was unfolding right in front of my eyes. *Just get out, Daria! Get free while you can!*

Inching up to my feet, I was finally able to suck in a full breath. I crept closer to the door, moving slowly so I wouldn't draw attention to myself, and winced when crunching glass broke beneath my shoes.

The gray wolf whipped his head in my direction. The black wolf still held my father by the throat. There was no blood, but my father's screams intensified while he thrashed beneath him.

I held up my hands. "Good boy." I didn't know what else to say. The gray wolf took a step toward me just as the air shimmered around the wolf holding my father.

The shimmer grew, as if the air became liquid, before the black wolf blurred in between the image of a man and a wolf. *What the . . .*

I blinked. My heart was pounding so hard that I thought I would pass out.

The shimmer vanished to reveal Logan crouched over my father, his shoulders heaving, his body naked. His mouth was still open by my dad's throat, but he shifted in an incredibly fast move so that his hands encircled my father's neck.

"Alexander!" Logan snarled. "Hold him!"

One of the gray-and-cream colored wolves leaped onto my father's chest just as my father tried to rise. The wolf's jaws locked around his neck once more, while the other two wolves moved in and bit into his legs, effectively pinning him in place.

Logan stood. His magnificent, chiseled body had my jaw dropping, but that wasn't the only reason.

"Did you just turn from a *wolf* to a human?" I shrieked. *Oh my god! This can't be happening!*

Logan's eyes glowed as he stepped toward me. I tried to keep my gaze on his face since his other parts—his very *male* parts—were on clear display. My lightheadedness grew stronger.

He didn't seem the least bit perturbed by his nudity. *Why should he? The dude just transformed from a wolf to a human!* Or perhaps I was imagining things. It was possible that my father had knocked me out and I was dreaming.

Short, shallow pants filled my chest. *I'm losing it!*

"Daria?" Logan said quietly. He stepped closer, a panicked look in his eyes. "Dar?" His gaze traveled over my face, hardening when he took in the details.

I was vaguely aware of something sticky running down my temple—probably more blood.

"Are you okay?"

He stepped closer, until his naked body pressed against mine. I closed my eyes and breathed in his scent. My heart slowed as his arms wrapped gently around me.

"Logan?" I whispered. "Is it really you?"

"Yeah, it's me."

My father's cries and the other wolves' snarls still filled the room.

Logan picked me up and moved us to the living room, then he set me down and looked me over. "He hit you." His jaw locked, the muscle ticking in the corner. "I should have been here. I didn't protect you."

I shook my head in wonder, still unable to believe what I'd witnessed only a few minutes ago, and considering the snarls and yelps coming from the back room, I hadn't imagined it, but it was not the time to ask questions or try to understand it.

"You couldn't have. I sneaked out before any of you woke. It was stupid. I shouldn't have done that."

His eyebrows drew together in a heavy scowl. "We'll talk about that later, but I still should have woken when you left. I should have heard you leave. I grew complacent." He shook his head. "Right now, I need to get you out of here."

In a blurred move, he swung me up in his arms, locking me against his chest. "Jake, Alexander, Brodie," he called over his shoulder. "Shift back and take him away. I want that bastard locked up."

Before I could ask what he meant by that, Logan strode toward the front door, kicked it open, and carried me out into the vast woods.

CHAPTER EIGHTEEN

Tree branches brushed against my face as birds chirped in the early-morning air. Logan carried me through the forest, as if it were the most normal thing in the world for a large naked male to carry a fully clothed, slightly beaten-up female through the woods.

A hysterical laugh bubbled up out of me. "What the hell happened back there? You can turn into a wolf?"

Logan winced at my tone. "Not a wolf. A werewolf."

"A *werewolf*? Is that somehow supposed to make sense?"

His lips twitched up for a second before he caught my expression. His smile faded. "Daria, it's okay. There are a lot of werewolves in the world."

"Really? There are a lot of werewolves in the world, and I'm supposed to just take that all in stride?"

His gaze softened. "I know it's a shock."

"Right, because until this morning, I had no idea." My brow furrowed, my mind spinning again. "And your friends are werewolves too? I heard you call for them back there, and there were three other wolves."

He nodded. "That's right. I'm a werewolf as are Jake, Brodie, and Alexander."

I let that information sink in. *He's a werewolf, his friends are werewolves, and I'm a supernatural healer.* Dizziness swam through me again. "Are you also going to tell me that there are more than just werewolves and healers? That there are vampires and gargoyles and all those other things that go bump in the night?"

"Well, yeah, if you want to get into it, all of those species exist, too, but there aren't many gargoyles. They're quite rare." He offered another tentative smile.

The blood drained from my face.

He cursed under his breath. "We'll get to that later. Why don't we just concentrate on you and me right now. You're a supernatural healer, or a witch if you want to be specific, and I'm a werewolf. End of story."

I squeezed my eyes tightly shut. *What the hell's happening?*

"Dar?" His arms tightened. "Just you and me, okay?"

Taking a deep breath, I met his steady gaze. His sandalwood scent wafted around me, and I took a few more breaths before nodding. "Right. Just you and me."

"I know this is new to you, so just take a minute. Keep breathing."

I closed my eyes and concentrated on inhaling and exhaling. His advice was sound. Without realizing it, I'd begun hyperventilating, but his calm tone and familiar scent helped push the anxiety down, and my head began to clear.

"Are you feeling better?" he asked a moment later.

I took another deep breath. "Yeah."

"If it helps, you can ask me about what I am."

An image of my father flashed through my mind. Only minutes ago, he'd thrown me against a wall. I shoved that memory down and asked in a rush, "So is that why your eyes glow? Because you're a werewolf?"

"You've seen my eyes glow?"

"Yeah, a few times. I thought I was seeing things, but apparently, I wasn't. Do they glow cause you're a wolf?"

He frowned. "All werewolves' eyes glow when we feel a heightened emotion. Normally, we hide it. Glowing eyes in public can cause problems." His frown grew. "But they glowed around you."

He shook his head, appearing troubled. I waited for him to explain that comment, but he suddenly seemed lost in his own thoughts.

Another moment of silence passed as I mulled over my new reality. Snapping twigs continued to fill the air as Logan walked steadily through the trees.

Another image rose unbidden in my mind. My father. His raised fist. His absolute hatred for me. I squeezed my eyes tightly shut. "So were you born a werewolf?" I opened my eyes again, just in time to see Logan duck us under a tree branch.

"Yes. I come from a long line of werewolves. My family descends from the originals, the world's first werewolves."

"That sounds impressive."

A deep groove appeared between his eyes. "I suppose it is," he replied, albeit reluctantly.

"And how many werewolves are in the world?"

His frown lessened, his gaze meeting mine again. "At last count, around fifteen thousand in the US, but there are more in other countries—maybe a hundred thousand worldwide. You really didn't know about us, did you?"

I shook my head.

"And your mom and grandma didn't know either?"

"Not that I know of. If they did, they never told me. But you knew about us?"

Logan sidestepped around an evergreen branch so it wouldn't scratch my face. The strong scent of pine wafted toward me. "The entire community knows about the Gresham women. The reason I answered your ad for a bodyguard was because supernaturals take care of their own."

"The entire community? What's that?"

"The supernatural community. We're an entire community of supes who live in the real world while disguising our true natures from the humans. Because we've been persecuted in the past, we've gone underground. Hiding hasn't stopped the SF's mission, though. Our job is to protect our own, but usually that's from other supes, not from one's human father." His tone hardened at the mention of my dad.

"SF?"

"Supernatural Forces."

"Is that supposed to mean something?" I brought a hand to my forehead and took a deep breath, concentrating on my breathing again. "Okay, lay it on me. What's the Supernatural Forces?"

That worried expression crossed Logan's features again, as if he wasn't sure if I was about to grow hysterical or not.

When I continued to look at him expectantly, he said slowly, "The Supernatural Forces is the supernatural community's version of the armed forces and law enforcement combined. My pack brothers and I are members."

"So you really *are* in the military?"

"I'm not in the US military, but yes, I'm in the supernatural one."

"And the part on your resume about personal security, when you said you've been working it for a few years, was that true or not?"

"Partly true. You're the first client I've taken on in a while to do bodyguard work for, but I have done it in the past."

"So that's why you never wanted to go to the police. Because you kinda are the police."

"Exactly."

I tried to lean back more in his arms, but my ribs ached, so I stopped. "I guess I'm lucky you saw my ad."

He ducked his head, even though there weren't any tree branches. "It wasn't luck. We've been keeping tabs on you."

My eyebrows rose. "What do you mean?"

"I mean that the SF monitors all supernaturals in an

attempt to prevent exactly what just happened back at your dad's mobile home. When we saw your ad, my boss put me on the job, and when you got that extortion email, I called it in. After I explained that your situation seemed more imminent than we'd originally thought, he agreed that more help was needed, so Brodie, Jake, and Alex were called in too."

"So that's what you meant when you said you'd need their help once my dad was found. You'd need them to help you arrest him?"

"Yeah, and now I'm doubly glad they were brought in, given what happened."

Since his tone hardened, I had a feeling that he still blamed himself for my father attacking me despite my sneaking away from the bus.

I grimaced. "What happened back there wasn't your fault. None of us knew my father was my stalker, and I shouldn't have left the bus like that. How can you do your job when your client sneaks out of your sight?"

"Actually, we *did* know it was your father. Alexander figured it out early this morning, a few hours before you left, after your dad clicked on one of the links. I was going to tell you first thing this morning, after I figured out how to break it to you, but when I woke up, you were gone. And then Cecile told me you were going to meet him—"

"I'm sorry. I shouldn't have done it. Looking back, I know it was so stupid, but I'd never thought it was him. How could somebody's own father do that?"

"Because he was desperate. He owed the mob money."

"The *mob?*" My head snapped back. *So that was who he owed money to.*

"It's probably why he attacked you. He wracked up quite the gambling debt and was running out of time. From what Alexander found on his computer, he originally had until the end of the month, but they upped his time-line. As of three days ago, he only had until the end of the week to come up with the money, and if he didn't . . ." Logan shrugged. "I'm sure you can guess what they'd do to him."

"That's why he went from threatening to kill me to demanding money. He probably wanted to scare me initially then work up to asking for money, but when he ran out of time, he attacked. But how did he get involved with the mob?"

"Gambling at the wrong places."

"So will they kill him now that he can't pay?"

"No. He'll be taken back to the SF. He saw too much. That will need to be fixed before he returns to the human world."

"Fixed." I brought a hand to my forehead, my breaths coming fast again. I could only imagine what that meant.

"Dar? It'll be okay. I promise."

Tears threatened to fill my eyes again, now that we were talking about my father. "So he was the one who dropped off the beheaded bird? If he's my stalker?"

Logan gritted his teeth. "Yeah, it was him. After Alexander got access to his computer, he learned all sorts of things, such as your father hacked your computer and your phone months ago. He's been tracking you ever since."

"Tracking me?"

"Through your cell's phone location. He knew where we were parked, and since we weren't far from his home the night before that show, what better time than to give you that present to scare you even more?"

"And that's how he knew that my clients' contact info was in my email. He's probably read all of those emails." When Logan looked at me quizzically, I explained how my father had planned to extort the money from me, by forcing my clients to put the money directly into his overseas account. A flush crept up my neck. "How can he hate me so much?"

"Because he's a deadbeat loser who doesn't deserve to share blood with you."

The anger in his voice made me wince, which caused my cheek to throb. I wished I had an icepack.

Logan's gaze darkened when he looked down and took in my injuries. I was pretty sure my face resembled a pulverized tomato. Not only had my father's shoves and smacks left me with a swollen cheek and nasty bruises blooming on both biceps, but I also had cuts on my head and dried blood on my face.

"I'll tend to your injuries as soon as we're back," he said.

"You don't have to. I'll be fine."

He growled, that predatory sound again. Since I knew he was a wolf, his grumblings and growls made a lot more sense.

"Do you mind if I pick up the pace?" he asked. "We're still a few miles from my clothes."

"Um, no. That's fine." It was on the tip of my tongue to tell him I could walk on my own despite my injuries, but that would have meant walking beside him, and he was completely nude. *Wonder what Crystal would think of that.*

Logan hefted me up higher in his arms. "I'll try to keep my run smooth. Let me know if it's not."

He took off. The force of his propulsion pushed me against his chest, his rock-hard abs pressing flush against my side. Wind flew over my cheeks as the trees around us turned into a blur.

I gasped as his legs pumped beneath us. The forest sounds continued, mostly the snapping branches and squishing ground as his bare feet landed on the uneven surface, but those sounds faded. Instead, Logan's steady rhythmic breathing filled my ears. Given how easily he breathed and moved, it didn't take a genius to figure out that he possessed inhuman strength and speed.

Duh, Dar. He's not human. He's a werewolf.

Only a few minutes passed before he stopped. He wasn't even winded.

"I'm going to set you down so I can get dressed."

I managed to nod before my body slid against his. He held onto me until I was standing steadily, then he turned and rummaged behind a rock.

My cheeks heated, and I quickly turned around. In that split second, I'd been awarded a very clear view of Logan's firm backside and broad back. His skin had a smooth, even complexion and was the color of honey.

I tried to calm my breathing as rustling came from behind me before the sound of his jeans zipping followed.

"The interstate is about two minutes away. We can cross it and call for a ride."

I tentatively turned around. Once again, my heart thumped.

He stood a few feet to the left, wearing his signature dark T-shirt and worn jeans. Mussed coffee-colored hair covered his head, and his eyes held a faint glow. I knew that meant he was feeling something, but I didn't know what.

"Does that mean we should walk that way?"

"I can carry you again if you'd like." He took a step closer to me.

I jumped back. "No, it's okay. I can walk, if you don't mind that I'm so slow."

His lips quirked up. "You're not that slow."

I smiled tentatively as he led the way through the trees. His unique scent wafted to me, and my senses swam. I still had so many questions for him, but at the moment, it took all of my concentration to not stare at the beautiful planes and muscles that were visible through his thin shirt.

Werewolf or not, my body still identified him as a potential mate.

CHAPTER NINETEEN

"Oh, thank the stars!" Cecile's thin arms locked around my neck the second I boarded the bus, but when she pulled back, her expression turned aghast. "Your face! What did he do to you?"

Logan didn't give me a chance to respond. "We need a first aid kit. Do you have one?"

Cecile waved toward the bathroom but didn't let me go. "In that back cabinet."

Logan strode to the back while Mike pulled his Yankees cap off and wiped a tear from his cheek. He hugged me, too, as soon as Cecile let go.

The feel of them caused electric jolts to run down my arms, but I did my best to push those sensations away. I even managed to squeeze Mike in return before I took a step back.

"We were so worried about you!" Cecile exclaimed.

"Especially after Logan and Alexander told us it was your father."

Up until that moment, I'd managed to push the horrific encounter with my father into the back of my mind. When Logan had carried me through the woods, everything he'd revealed distracted me from the horrors I'd experienced only an hour ago, but now that I was back at home, safe with those I loved . . .

Tears filled my eyes.

Cecile settled me down on the couch. "It's okay, Dar. We're all here. You're safe now."

Logan returned, rifling through the contents of the kit before pulling out antiseptic and bandages.

His sandalwood and forest scent flooded my senses. I inhaled. Just his presence calmed the panic in my chest. Using careful touches, he cleaned the blood off my face, applied salve, and bandaged the cut on my forehead.

Mike retrieved a bag of ice from the kitchen while Cecile fluffed pillows around me. Once I was cleaned up, Cecile asked tentatively, "What happened?"

I wrung my hands, my lip trembling.

"We arrived in time," Logan cut in. I gave him a grateful smile. He went on to explain what my father had done and why. When he got to the part about finding me on the floor with my father looming over me, Mike sucked in a breath, and Cecile gasped.

Mike shook his head in disgust. "Smart thinking to text us his address, Dar. If you hadn't, Logan and his friends wouldn't have found you."

Logan's jaw locked. "He's right. Your scent wasn't easy to track, and the address we found for Dillon was wrong."

"Scent?" Cecile's eyebrows rose.

I sucked in a breath when Logan stiffened, then I forced myself to relax, remembering how trustworthy Mike and Cecile were. "You can tell them. Your secret will be safe."

Mike cocked his head. "What secret?"

Logan took a deep breath, the couch dipping more in his direction with the movement. "Brodie, Alexander, and Jake are my pack brothers. We're werewolves."

It grew so quiet that you could hear a pin drop.

"Come . . . come again?" Cecile stuttered.

"I'm not the only supernatural." I sat up straighter.

Though I couldn't be sure, it felt like Logan shifted closer to me, almost protectively.

"According to Logan, there's an entire community of people like me, but I never knew about them."

Cecile's jaw dropped. Mike merely swallowed, his eyes as round as saucers.

"So you can turn into a wolf?" Cecile's hand fluttered to her hair.

I nudged Logan. "How about you show them?"

USING A DRAPED towel for modesty's sake, Logan shifted four times between wolf and human while Cecile and Mike peppered him with questions in between. As for me, I merely enjoyed seeing Logan with his shirt off even though in the back of my mind I knew I shouldn't. He was still my employee. He still had a girlfriend, and only that morning, he'd held me in his arms . . . naked.

And I'd loved every minute of it.

When Cecile and Mike's amazement finally subsided, Logan retreated to the back to dress properly.

Mike cleared his throat when Logan walked back out. "Speaking of your . . . uh, pack brothers. Where are they now?"

I stiffened at the reminder of how we'd left Brodie, Jake, and Alexander. They'd had Dillon pinned to the floor.

Logan joined me on the couch again. "They're probably halfway back to Boise by now with Daria's father in tow. Boise is where our headquarters are stationed."

"So they arrested Dillon?" I asked.

I couldn't stomach referring to Dillon as my father anymore. That man wasn't my dad. He was a monster. I shifted uncomfortably despite the feel of Logan brushing up against me. Once again, he sat closer than he needed to.

"You could say that. The guys are bringing him to the community to be dealt with. We have a few sorcerers that handle situations like this. They'll scramble Dillon's brain and wipe any memory of our existence from his mind. Following that, he'll be doused in a heady potion that will have him cowering in the corner if he so much as thinks of coming near you again."

"You mean he'll be brainwashed?" Cecile clutched her throat.

Logan shrugged. "Something like that. But the important thing is that he won't be bothering Daria anymore."

I took a deep unsteady breath. So much had happened in the past few hours.

"I still can't believe it." Cecile hung her head. "The entire time, it was *him*. And now it all makes sense, why your mother never spoke of him and cringed anytime I brought him up." Tears shone in her eyes when they met mine. "He was always so charming the few times I met him, but then one day, he was just . . . gone. Your mom never spoke about him again."

A lump formed in my throat at the mention of my mother.

Mike shook his head in disgust. "That man doesn't deserve to be called your father, and he never deserved your mother's affection, even if he was a potential mate."

I covered his hand with mine. "No, but you do. You're the one who's been here for me my entire life, Mike. You and Cecile. You're both like parents to me."

His gaze shot up. Tears moistened his eyes.

I removed my hand when the tingles became too much to bear, but the lump in my throat remained.

Cecile dabbed at her eyes. "And you're safe now, Dar. That's all that matters since Dillon is being taken care of." Her gaze turned back to Logan. "You *are* going to take care of him, right? Like you said, he won't be a threat to Daria anymore?"

Logan's eyes softened when he glanced down at me. "That's right. He'll never hurt her again. I'll personally guarantee that."

CHAPTER TWENTY

Cecile canceled my show that afternoon while Logan spent most of his time on the phone.

I caught snippets of his conversation. From the sounds of it, I gathered that Logan was leaving the next day for a new job.

Words like *yes, sir* and *assignment* came up once or twice. That in itself made my heart pound, but when I overheard details about his upcoming new job, a job that involved dragons and a part-time SF member who also trained dragons for her other job, my mind spun.

Is this really the world I've always lived in?

It seemed too much to take in.

I rearranged myself on the couch and curled my legs beneath me. My cheek throbbed from where Dillon had hit me, the skin tender and pink. Logan had applied a few butterfly bandages to various cuts on my arms and face, but other than that, I wasn't overly injured, minus the numerous bruises.

I gazed out the bus's windows. Another rest stop waited in front of us. Mike had driven us to central Montana following the incident with my father. My next tour stop was around the area, but we were running behind, thanks to Dillon Parker.

We planned to resume business as usual the next day. Hopefully, the cuts and bruises on my face wouldn't attract too much attention. Although, most likely, a good layer of foundation would cover all of it.

I curled my fingers around the sofa cushion at the thought of performing—of healing people. Thinking about the amount of energy that would take made my stomach heave.

I didn't even want to consider how disappointed my clients that I canceled on were. Once again, I'd let them down.

Who knows if we'll be able to work them into the schedule or not.

But at the moment, performing wasn't an option. Cecile had insisted on that, and after initially arguing with her, I'd come to agree.

I'd been fine when Logan had revealed his wolf form to Cecile and Mike. I'd even laughed a few times. My mood had been okay, even good, but now, Logan was leaving soon because his job was done, and inside . . .

It was another story.

Everything was catching up with me.

Twice that morning, while Logan was on the phone, Mike was driving us to the new rest stop, and Cecile was rearranging my schedule, I'd had moments when I couldn't breathe. Memories of my father advancing on me kept assaulting my mind.

A raised fist.

That dark look.

My own father had turned on me. Someone of my own flesh and blood had viewed me as an abomination, as something the world was better off without.

One side of me knew that Dillon's actions didn't reflect anything about my character. But every time I thought about what he had done to me, or how my entire view of the world had shattered after what Logan revealed about the community, my breath stopped.

And on top of that, even though Dillon had never been a real father to me, the crushing understanding that I would *never* have a biological father was a new devastating blow. My dreams as a little girl of finding the long-lost father who loved me would always be just that—dreams.

How can I keep it together enough to do my job tomorrow?

By late afternoon, I couldn't take it anymore. I flew out of the bus and into the warm sun. Logan's dark eyes flashed my way while he held his cell phone to his ear.

"Daria!" Cecile yelled, but I didn't stop.

My feet slapped on the pavement as I sprinted from our home, across the parking lot. Traffic from I-90 hummed in the background. A blaring semi. The whiz of cars.

But I didn't pay it any attention.

My life had been turned upside down and inside out. Nothing in our world was what I'd thought it was, and my father hated me enough that he would rather use me for money than see me alive.

The wind flew through my long hair when I leaped onto the sidewalk. A few bystanders' jaws dropped as I raced past them. I felt certain that my choked sobs and the tears streaming down my beat-up face had something to do with that.

Hot air burned in my lungs as I ran past the rest stop building. *Just run! Just get out of here!*

Behind the rest stop loomed mountainous terrain. Jutting rocks scattered with pine trees and dry grass rose from the ground like stalagmites.

I raced up a forested hill, falling forward on my hands at times when the terrain grew so steep that I couldn't stay upright. Twigs and rocks cut into my face and palms, but I didn't slow.

Ragged breathing and my cries of pain filled the air as I climbed the steep foothill. I was losing it. A part of my mind was aware of that, but I didn't stop.

It wasn't until I reached the top of the steep hill that I collapsed to the ground. Gasping sobs, oscillating between cries of pain and howls of anger, shook my chest as I lay in the dirt, my fingers curling into the dry ground littered with pine needles and rocks.

"How could he?" I punched the ground. "My own father! How could he?"

Memories kept assaulting me, making everything worse.

My mother.

Her smile.

Her laugh.

More than ever I wanted her beside me. I wanted her to tell me that it wasn't me. It wasn't us. That there was nothing we could have ever done to make my father love us.

But she was gone and never coming back. A deep, keening wail parted my lips. *I want you here, Mom! I want you here!*

It wasn't until warm hands touched my back that I became aware of Logan's presence.

"Daria," he whispered and turned me around.

Twigs snapped, and a breeze caressed my wet cheeks. His warm hands and intoxicating scent swam through my senses and had me gripping his shirt tightly. The feel of the smooth cotton beneath my fingertips and the rumble of Logan's chest as he spoke words I struggled to understand eventually broke through my grief-ridden state.

I kneeled on the ground, immobile and panting, as a deep glow filled his eyes.

"Your hands," he murmured.

I looked down. Through the tears blurring my vision, blood was visible on my palms. My panicked scramble up the hill had only done more damage to my body.

"I . . ." I brought a shaky hand up to my head. Leaves stuck to my hair.

He gently pulled the leaves out, the glow in his eyes intensifying. "I'm sorry I didn't pay more attention to how you were feeling. I knew this would come. Trauma always creates a reaction in everyone. I shouldn't have been on the phone. I should have been more attentive to you."

His whispered words had me leaning forward, wanting to melt into him, but at the last moment, I pulled myself upright.

What are you doing, Dar?

It was bad enough that Logan was seeing me in such a state, but then to throw myself at him, especially when he had a girlfriend was ten times worse.

Pull it together!

I concentrated on the feel of the dry earth beneath my knees, using that to ground me.

Logan pulled a small twig from my hair, that glow still in his eyes. "Do you want to talk about it?"

For a moment, I didn't say anything, but then I replied in an acid tone, "What's there to talk about? My own father would rather have seen me hurt than in his life, and all he ever wanted from me was money." I shook my head. "I'm such a fool. The way he acted last night when we had dinner, like he cared—it was all fake. That was just a ruse to get me alone so he could steal from me, and I was stupid enough to fall for it."

Logan's jaw tightened. "You're not a fool, and you know his actions have nothing to do with you. He's a sick bastard. That doesn't reflect on you." He leaned down and whispered in my ear, "You know that, right?"

The feel of his sweet breath puffing so close to my skin made my eyes close. I licked my lips. "I know. I've been telling myself that, but . . ."

He pulled back, not far but just enough so I could see his eyes again. They still glowed. "It doesn't feel that way? You feel like there must be something wrong with you for your own father to act that way?"

I squeezed my eyes shut again. Tears sprouted from them despite my trying to hold them back. "Yes."

"Fuck." Abruptly, Logan pulled me toward him, and my body planted against his hard chest. His arms locked around me, his scent everywhere. "It's not you! It's not. I've dealt with hundreds of assholes like him. And I know you doubt yourself right now. I know you feel that some part of this must be your fault, but it's not." He growled, the low rumble filling his chest. "If you had any idea how amazing you are. I've never met someone who cares so much about those around her. Someone who risks her own life to save others and doesn't give a second thought about putting her own life in harm's way. That's not somebody any normal person would hate. Your dad's messed up, and you're simply the innocent daughter who got caught up in his lies."

Shivers ran through my body at the feel of his steel-like arms around me.

"You blow my mind, Daria Gresham," he whispered softly. "My wolf knew something was special about you the moment we met, and the thought of you doubting yourself because some sicko tried to take something from you—" His voice grew tight as another discontented growl rumbled in his chest. "I want to kill him for doing that to you, because you're the absolute last person who deserves anything like that."

My breath caught as I peered up at him. Tears still clouded my vision. "Do you mean all of that? Not just the stuff about my father, but about what you think of . . . me?"

The glow in his eyes increased, making his chocolate irises turn gold. Even with the bright sunshine streaming through the trees around us, I could see it.

"I meant every word of it." He tucked a strand of hair behind my ear. A soft breeze rustled through the trees. I shivered, but it had nothing to do with the wind.

"And Crystal, I mean your girlfriend, won't mind you saying those things to me?"

His gaze narrowed. "Just what do you know about Crystal?"

"I saw a text she sent you. Just one," I said in a rush. "I didn't mean to pry, but I saw a few words from it, and I heard you guys talking about her outside the bus by that magic shop."

A long moment passed before his gaze shifted and he broke eye contact. "Crystal's not my girlfriend."

My lips parted. "She's not?"

"No."

Elation coursed through me so swift and strong that I feared I might pass out. "So you don't have a girlfriend?"

Another moment passed, his gaze still averted. "No."

"Then who's Crystal?"

His nostrils flared, his gaze staying over my shoulder. "A girl from back home."

But not his girlfriend . . .

Before I knew what I was doing, I pushed myself against him more, my breasts squashing on his chest. The need to be with him, to touch him, was so strong. I didn't know if it was because he was a potential mate or if my feelings were real, but at the moment, I didn't care. I wanted him. I *needed* him. I wanted to wrap myself up in him and forget everything that had happened that morning.

"Touch me," I whispered.

He groaned, his breath coming faster. "Dar, you're vulnerable right now."

"I'm not."

"You are." He tensed, trying to pull back, but I gripped him tighter, not letting him retreat.

"Logan," I breathed. He didn't have a girlfriend, and he was a potential mate. My blood felt on fire for him.

"Dar . . ." he replied, his tone low and warning. Every muscle in his body tightened, veins popping beneath the skin. He closed his eyes. Even his cheek muscles appeared strained. "Damn, woman. I'm trying so hard to control myself right now. I don't want to take advantage of you. I don't want to lose control."

"I want you to lose control," I whispered.

"Fuck, Daria." He groaned then pulled me against him so hard my head spun.

His lips locked against mine in a bruising kiss as my breasts crushed against his chest.

I wrapped my arms tightly around his neck and locked my legs around his waist.

His hands cupped my ass and pulled me even tighter to him.

Instinct took over as I grinded against him. Despite my bruised cheek and sore ribs, I met his demanding embrace as heat grew so strongly in my core that I felt like an inferno. Tingles of pleasure shot along my limbs as his tongue plunged into my mouth.

I'd never tasted anybody in a kiss before, and I didn't want it to end. Our bodies molded into one, and the feel of his rock-hard arms locked around me felt right on every single level.

It felt like I'd come home.

He tore his mouth away and pressed urgent kisses down my neck. I arched my back, tilting my head to give him better access.

He groaned when my breasts strained against my shirt, which was pulling down because it had caught on his waistband, creating a deep V. My cleavage swelled over the material.

"Damn, woman," he breathed. He pulled my shirt up and over my head before I could blink.

Warm air washed across my bare skin, making my flesh pebble. Desire pulsed low and hard in my belly, making me squirm more. My hands automatically reached behind my back to unclasp my bra.

When it came undone, my breasts spilled out of the sides. I held the thin material over the front of my peaks.

Logan's ragged breathing filled the forest as his eyes glowed so brightly that I couldn't tell where his pupils ended and his irises began.

His hard length, pushing against his jeans, grew harder. "Daria," he said in a ragged voice. "I want you."

"I want you too." I let my bra fall to the side. Warm summer air swirled over my naked chest, but my nipples acted like they were in the arctic. They stood tall and proud, as ripe as cherries on a tree, ready for the picking.

"Holy shit, you're beautiful." His hands came up to cup my boobs before he leaned down and drew one hard bud into his mouth.

I cried out as foreign sensations coursed through my body. Never had I felt so alive or wanted a man so much. I grinded against his crotch more as a deep, aching need grew inside me.

His erection grew, and the feel of Logan's warm mouth and tantalizing tongue sucking my breasts created an aching swell to rise higher and higher inside me.

He released one arm to lock around my waist as his mouth sucked and fondled my tits. Using his free arm, he pushed me more firmly onto his erection, grinding me against his hard length. Even though we both still wore our jeans, I responded, bucking against him.

When his tongue flicked my nipple at the same time his cock tried to penetrate me through his denim, I lost control.

My head fell back as an orgasm wracked my entire body in wave after wave of pleasure. He continued to suck one peak then the other, as if his mouth couldn't decide which tit he wanted more. His unrelenting tongue only made my release more intense.

When my orgasm finally subsided, I sank into his arms like jelly. His harsh breaths filled my ears as he held me tightly to him.

His firm erection still pressed against me, and from his trembling arms and sweaty face, I knew he was still incredibly aroused and wanted more.

I peeked up at him. His eyes glowed so brightly they swirled like liquid gold. "I . . ." I cleared my throat. "I've never done that before."

His eyes widened for the merest second as he panted. "You've never had an orgasm before?"

I dipped my gaze sheepishly. My naked boobs still pressed against his fully clothed chest. "Actually, um, none of this. I've never had an orgasm, and I . . ." I groaned and brought a hand up to cover my eyes. "I've never done *any* of this before. You're the first guy I've kissed."

His whole body grew rigid.

I tensed, my insides growing cold. It suddenly struck me that being a virgin wasn't always the most attractive quality to some men.

"Are you kidding me?" One of his calloused fingers tilted my chin up, his breathing still ragged. With his other hand, he forced my hand away from my face so I had to look him in the eye. "This is the first time you've ever fooled around with a guy?"

"I've tried before but was never able to tolerate it." Tears of humiliation burned my eyes. I tried to pull my chin away, but he wouldn't let me. "It's my gift. I can't . . ." Tears fell onto my cheeks. "I can't touch. Not like normal people. My healing light goes haywire, and I just . . . can't," I finished lamely.

He wiped my tears away, being careful to avoid my tender cheek. "But you can with me?" The glow in his eyes intensified.

I sniffed. "Yeah. With you I can."

A contented growl filled his chest as a satisfied smile spread across his face.

I wiped my eyes as the tears abated. "So that doesn't bother you?"

He laughed. Actually *laughed* which had my jaw dropping. "Does it bother me that no other guy has gotten you off in his lap before?" Another chuckle rumbled his chest. "I'm sorry to disappoint you, Miss Gresham, but my wolf and I are over the moon that nobody else has had you."

"So you don't mind that I'm a virgin?"

"Even if you weren't a virgin, I'd still want you, but the fact that no guy has ever seen you like this or touched your amazing body makes me want to claim you even more."

"Claim me?"

"It's a wolf thing."

I cocked my head. His statement reminded me how much my life had changed in the past twelve hours. Logan was a werewolf. An entire community of supernaturals existed, and I was one of them.

"So what exactly does that mean, that you want to claim me?" A thrill ran through me at how possessive that sounded.

His eyes, which had returned to a chocolate brown, glowed again. "It means my wolf wants to claim you even more. He wants to mark you as ours before another wolf can beat us to it. Virgins in the werewolf world are highly revered. Not many women are still virgins when they're marked. You know, since casual sex is pretty common in today's world, and women are just as free as men to taste what's out there."

"You make it sound like a mating thing."

"It is."

My mouth parted. "Is that like . . . marriage or something in the werewolf world?"

The corner of his mouth tilted up. "Something like that, but don't freak out. Since there are no wolves in the vicinity, I won't be dragging you down the aisle quite yet."

My cheeks heated at how casually he spoke of our future, but any excitement over tantalizing encounters to come was doused when I realized what tomorrow brought. "You're still leaving tomorrow. Is your wolf okay with that?"

He swallowed tightly. "I have to go. There's an assignment that the boys and I have to tend to, but lucky for you, my wolf doesn't make the decisions. I do. Otherwise, I'd have you up against a tree right now while we rut right here in the open." He laughed when he caught my expression. Leaning closer to my ear, he whispered, "Don't worry. Our first time will be the most arousing and mind-blowing experience you've ever had. As much as my wolf wants to claim you right now, I'm going to make sure that when I take your virginity it's an experience that you'll never forget."

I shivered as a tingle raced down my spine. His cock hardened beneath me again, as if sensing how easily he aroused me.

"Then you'll be mine and mine alone," he added.

My breaths came faster as the implications of his statement sank in. *His? His alone?*

He just chuckled more, probably from my overwhelmed expression.

A smile curved my lips. "You could have told me that right away. I thought my virginity offended you."

Since the topic between us had shifted from sex to my virginity, I picked my discarded bra up off the ground and brushed it off.

Logan frowned when I hooked it back on, his face growing so crestfallen that *I* laughed.

"Do you have to do that?" He looked like a sullen teenager who'd just had his Xbox taken away.

I swiveled my head around, my cheeks suddenly flushing at where we were and what we'd done. "What if someone climbs up here and sees us?"

His eyebrows shot up, his expression amused. "Have you noticed where we are? There's no trail coming up here.

You took off into the mountains and forged your own path." He shifted beneath me, and I grew aware of his massive erection again.

"Oh!" I squealed.

He rubbed against me more, and a flush stained my cheeks.

"Did you want me to . . . I mean, I don't know how to, but I can try . . ." I fumbled with his jeans.

His hand abruptly covered mine. "It's okay. I think I've taken advantage of you enough for one day. I didn't mean for it to go this far, but when you got your glorious tits out . . ." He sighed and raked a hand through his hair. "I'll control myself better next time."

Next time.

My insides sang with happiness. "Does that mean I'll see you soon?" I asked hesitantly.

"I'd like that. I want to show you the supernatural community and introduce you to our way of life."

My heart beat harder, thundering against my ribs. "You do?"

"Yeah. I want to take you there."

I glanced down. My breaths were coming so fast. More than anything, I wanted to touch him. I wanted to press my hands against his body and feel his muscles jump and respond, but a crashing realization had me stiffening against him.

Logan and I led two separate lives. As much as I hated it, his life was in the supernatural one, and mine was in the human one. *My clients are counting on me. They'll die if I leave.*

"What are you thinking?" He tilted my chin up with a calloused finger.

My lips parted, my tongue darting out to lick them. His gaze dipped, his pupils dilating. I shook myself, trying to control the animalistic urge to melt my body against his.

I pulled back, putting more distance between us. "I was thinking that we lead different lives. I can't even fathom growing up as you have. My entire life, I thought I was unique, but I'm not, and there's an entire world within my world that I didn't even know about."

"So you can come with me," he said hesitantly. "Come with me tomorrow and join me in my world. It's the world you should be living in. Not this one."

Tears pricked my eyes again, making my vision blur. "But I can't. I want to, but I can't, Logan."

His eyes glowed brighter, his grip tightening. "Why can't you?"

"People are counting on me. My job provides for Cecile and Mike, and I still have to finish this tour, and in a few months, we'll start another one. I have a wait list that's years long. If I leave . . ." My breath caught.

He sighed angrily. "Your clients will die."

"Yes."

Neither of us said anything after that admission. The forest breeze continued to flutter around us, and chipmunks chattered in the trees. Logan's chest warmed against me. The anguish in his eyes had me placing my palms on his shoulders and scooting closer.

His arms automatically locked around my waist. "I don't want to leave you."

Hope rose so strongly and swiftly in my chest that my voice turned breathless. "Then don't. You can stay with *me*." I didn't breathe as I waited for his reply.

He leaned forward until our foreheads touched. "I can't. People are counting on me too."

In the distance, the faint hum of traffic filtered up from the valley where the interstate ran. That sound only reminded me that my life was waiting at the bottom of the hill—a life I was suddenly unsure if I wanted.

But I had promises to keep.

"When do you have to go?" Fresh pain cut through my soul as the scent of pine wafted up around us. I wiggled closer to him. I couldn't get close enough as reality set in.

He groaned when I settled on his crotch. My eyes flashed wide open when I felt his hard length through his jeans. He was so *big*.

"I have a bus ticket for ten in the morning." He closed his eyes as a muscle ticked in his jaw. "Even though leaving you is the last thing I want to do."

CHAPTER TWENTY-ONE

The smell of diesel hung in the air. Behind us, a rumbling Greyhound bus collected passengers at the McDonald's in Miles City.

We waited outside since Logan would be leaving on it in fifteen minutes. Gray clouds filled the sky, rain in the forecast.

Logan was on his phone a dozen yards away, pacing as he hashed out work details for his next assignment. Cecile, Mike, and I hung back. A sharp lump formed in my throat as I watched him.

Logan had saved me from Dillon Parker, a man who should have loved me—a man who was currently being processed in the SF's holding facility in Boise.

Chills ran down my spine as I remembered how easily Dillon had gained access to my computer—and discovered everything and anything about me—but according to

Logan, in a few days, Dillon's memory would be wiped clean of me and his hacking skills.

His computer equipment had already been confiscated, and according to Logan, from now until the day he died, Dillon would struggle to know how to turn a computer on, much less how to hack into someone else's.

As for the mob . . . well, I imagined Dillon had what was coming to him in the human world when he returned.

I shivered even though I knew I would never have to worry about Dillon Parker again—all because Logan Smith had come into my life.

"You'll see Logan again." Cecile patted my hand. "Something tells me *that* one will be back."

I gave a slight nod, the lump in my throat too big for me to speak.

I'd told Cecile the previous night that Logan didn't have a girlfriend, after he and I had returned to the bus, but even though I still wasn't entirely sure who Crystal was to Logan, I trusted him.

If he said he didn't have a girlfriend, I believed him.

"And there are only two weeks left in your tour," she added, "then you can visit him. Meeting other people like you would be good for you."

"She's right, Dar," Mike added. "You should meet more people your age. People like you."

I swallowed the lump down and forced a smile. "Are you saying I should try to make more friends?"

Mike raised his hands, as if in surrender. "Who? Me? Did I say that?"

I laughed lightly, genuinely, some of the tension easing from my lips.

Cecile smiled. "Your entire life we've been trying to help you connect with people your age. You may meet some young people there who understand you better than we ever could."

My smile vanished, my brows furrowing. "You've always understood me, Cece. And you, too, Mike. Even though only Mom and Nan knew what it was like to live with magic and light, that hasn't stopped either of you from trying to understand and make my life easier."

Cecile squeezed my hand briefly but let go before the tingles started. "You're like a daughter to me, Daria. I know I can never replace your mom, but to me, you're the daughter I never had." She smoothed her hair, taming the few stray tendrils that had escaped her bun. "I just want you to know that, because something tells me all of our lives are going to change in the next few months."

Before I could ask her what she meant, Logan was striding back to us.

My breath caught in my throat at the stormy look in his dark eyes. His T-shirt clung to his muscled chest, and his hard thighs were visible through his jeans. His gaze landed on mine and held it.

Mike checked his watch. "We need to get moving so we're not late. Your show starts in two hours, Dar. As much as I hate to say it, this goodbye will have to be quick."

Cecile checked her watch too. "My stars. You're right! We need to get moving."

Logan stopped a few feet away. I tilted my head back to meet his eyes.

"Logan, we can't thank you enough," Cecile said. "You kept our girl safe and have taken care of that horrible man."

Mike held out his hand for Logan to shake. "I second everything Cecile said." He pumped Logan's hand up and down. "Safe travels to you, Logan. I hope we see you again."

Logan's attention flicked back to me. "You can count on that."

A shiver ran through me at his adamant response.

"Well . . . we'll just . . ." Cecile pried Mike's hand away from Logan's. "We'll be on the bus and ready to go. Take a few minutes, Dar, then we'll be on our way."

Cecile guided Mike back to our bus as more passengers stepped onto the Greyhound.

Logan dipped his head down. "You have my number?"

I nodded. "It's saved in my phone."

"Good. I'll call you tonight after your show, if you're not too tired to talk."

Tears threatened to fill my eyes, but I blinked them back. *Damn, this is harder than I thought it would be.* "Text me when you get there?" I shoved my hands into my back jean pockets since they were trembling.

He growled and stepped closer until my breasts brushed against his chest. His gaze dipped down, and a faint glow lit the halo around his irises.

Tingles shot through me, as a rush of desire flamed.

Logan's nostrils flared. "I can smell your arousal." He

put his hands around my waist and pulled me flush against him.

I pulled my hands free from my pockets and locked my arms around his neck. "You can? What does it smell like?"

He dipped his head and whispered in my ear, "Like you, but sweeter with a hint of musk." He inhaled deeply, burying his nose into my neck. "You smell like roses in heat."

The feel of his breath puffing against my neck made my knees go weak. Even though I had no idea what he was talking about regarding my scent, I didn't care. Just the feel of him was enough to make me picture us on the hill again. More than anything, I wanted to rip his shirt off. "When will I see you next?"

"A week or two? I'm heading straight to work when I get home. I'm not sure how long our next job will take, but I'll come back as soon as I'm free, or you can come to me when your tour ends."

I nodded rapidly and leaned into his neck, inhaling his sandalwood scent. "Is it dangerous? Where you're going?"

"I'll stay safe."

My stomach churned at his evasive response. "I'll miss you."

"I'll miss you too," he said gruffly, tipping my chin up. "Come here."

He molded his lips to mine, his scent exploding around me. I clung to him as his tongue parted my lips. Unable to stop myself, I moaned. A low growl filled his chest, vibrating against me.

When he finally pulled back, the Greyhound driver was calling for any remaining passengers to board.

"You'd better go." I still had my arms locked around him.

"Easier said than done." He kissed me again before leaning into my neck to inhale. "I want to remember your scent, especially when you're aroused like this."

My stomach flipped as I curled my fingers through his hair.

He squeezed me one last time before letting go. "I'll see you soon."

"Bye, Logan."

He turned and walked away.

The parting image of his lean hips and broad shoulders seared into my mind as hot as a brand.

Even though I knew I would see him soon, a deep aching fear grew that it wouldn't be enough, that our lives weren't meant to be together, that our situations would forever keep us apart.

I could only hope that I was wrong, because I knew one thing with absolute certainty—I'd fallen head over heels in love with Logan Smith, and I *wanted* to find a way to be with him.

BOOK TWO
SUPERNATURAL COMMUNITY

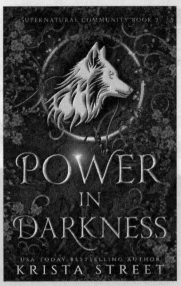

Turns out, I'm not the only supernatural in the world . . . My new werewolf boyfriend, Logan Smith, wants to introduce me to the supernatural community—a secret society of magical species that live in hiding in the human world.

But my introduction doesn't go as planned.

On the night before my arrival, a terrifying event births a new power inside me. It's cold, powerful, and worst of all, I lose my livelihood overnight since I can't touch anyone now without killing them.

Now as I enter the community, while terrified of hurting innocents, I learn that to stop the dark power I must dig into my family's past to uncover the truth of who I really am.

Thankfully, I have Logan to help me along the way. Not only is he sinfully delicious, but he's loyal, trustworthy, and is committed to staying at my side. Or so I thought . . .

ABOUT THE AUTHOR

Krista Street loves writing in multiple genres: fantasy, sci-fi, romance, and dystopian. Her books are cross-genre and often feature complex characters, plenty of supernatural twists, and romance in every story. She loves writing about coming-of-age characters who fight to find their place in this world while also finding their one true mate.

Krista Street is a Minnesota native but has lived throughout the U.S. and in another country or two. She loves to travel, read, and spend time in the great outdoors. When not writing, Krista is either chasing her children, spending time with her husband and friends, sipping a cup of tea, or enjoying the hidden gems of beauty that Minnesota has to offer.

THANK YOU

Thank you for reading *Magic in Light,* book one in the *Supernatural Community* series.

If you enjoy Krista Street's writing, make sure you visit her website to learn about her new release text alerts, newsletter, and other series.

www.kristastreet.com

Links to all of her social media sites are available on every page.

Last, if you enjoyed reading *Magic in Light,* please consider logging onto the retailer you purchased this book from to post a review. Authors rely heavily on readers reviewing their work. Even one sentence helps a lot. Thank you so much if you do!